Frankie Takes a Dive

Cooperative Realm

Nicky Penttila

Book Cover by John A. Spillane

Illustrations by Envato

Published by Wondrous Publishing

I

Frankie Takes a Dive

Chapter One

She wasn't the kind to willingly spend time with the riff-raff, so the shuttle from Shepherd Orbital Space Station to the platform nearest to Valdes Underwater Resort was murder.

Rosing System Superior Court Judge Aino Miller did not suffer fools. But apparently, only fools took this ancient, airplane-shaped shuttle in the middle of this brutish, backward, planet's day.

Her own fault, she supposed, watching the alleged human next to her handle some sticky neon green food substance while simultaneously dragging their fingers across their portable device. But Aino had refused to rise early today. It wasn't a vacation if she had to travel at some blasted groggy hour. She did plenty enough of that for work.

She shifted closer to the wall of the shuttle, trying to avoid splatter. Aino always demanded a window seat. She closed her eyes, ignored the weird cheese odor wafting over the seat in front of her, and called up in imagination the images from the brochure.

Two full days to roam the sturdy tubes and spacious pods of the sector's biggest undersea playground. To eat terrific meals while scores of multihued fish watched enviously from the other side of triple-reinforced windows. Swim with the colorful fish in strictly supervised safety conditions. Pet a dolphin! Really a rosicant, this planet's version of a dolphin, only furrier.

All of that was what everybody—every superior body— enjoyed at Valdes Underwater Resort. What the resort was offering her, and no more than a dozen similarly discerning, deep-pocketed clients, was something special.

Aino had heard about it from a close friend, but of course had done her own due diligence. The place was legit. The owner, Monica Valdes, was a hands-on person who somehow still maintained a shockingly clean legal record.

In addition, Valdes had managed to make the introductions to previous attendees in a way that Aino could ask them about the experience without either party giving away their identities. Quite clever.

And the cover story was a logical one, in a world filled with fools.

Aino left her shuttle companions to haul themselves and their slop into the arrivals terminal. Valdes Resort had an air limo ready and waiting for her directly on the landing platform. She was its only passenger.

The ten-minute trip to the beach was dull. Row upon row of stunted brown tree-things whipped back and forth in the planet's scirocco winds. She didn't feel it; the limo must be reinforced. No people, until they neared the beach, where a narrow town hid behind parallel windbreaks.

Aino had expected to transfer to a hopper at the beach to get to the resort itself. Limos were less reliable over water. But her limo took her the entire way. From the white sands on the edge of

Dorian Bay and into the bay itself: a tube wide enough for two-way wheeled traffic. Once past the docks and such, the upper half of the tube went transparent. The underwater adventure started even before she arrived.

Smart. Impressed despite herself at the number of different fish even this close to land, Aino almost didn't notice the progressive increase in air pressure as the car descended. Then her ears started to pop. She wriggled her jaw, and the pressure quickly eased. The rest of her body didn't feel any different, buckled loosely into a velvety bench seat.

The drive down was sedate—almost enough time to count all the fish—but the return trip on Sunday would take eight times as long. The resort guaranteed that guests who followed its depressurizing routine would not get the bends when returning to shore. Must be what they used those half-domed cul-de-sac turnoffs on the sides of the road for. Waiting out the pressure.

Did the air already taste different? The brochure said the mix at the resort, 194.3 meters from the surface, was "near-normal" for standard air-breathing humans. The scent reminded her of the gas they used on kids who were frightened of booster shots. Helium.

A shadow passing overhead caught her attention. One of those furry porpoises—rosicants—had streaked over the top of the tube. Silver and black, long nose and thick-rocket body, it shot straight down the side, its wicked tail passing out of view at the bottom edge of the window. The bruised-green tips of swaying plants peeking up from the underside swayed out of view for a moment as the big fish passed. Must be hungry.

When Aino looked forward again, her breath caught. She hadn't realized how steep this tube-road really was.

Still far below sat a dome the diameter of a sodding level of the orbital station she'd just left. Thousands of people could fit in there, each in separate rooms. And it wasn't the only dome. To one side ran a collection of far-shorter round-top buildings, most connected by tubes to make hexagons, some off on a tube of their own. A living organic molecule diagram.

Opposite that side, the resort sat hard upon the edge of a chasm, its waters a blackened blue. Perfect for deep diving, the brochure said, but the thing looked blasted dangerous to her.

Good for orientation, though. The VIP area was only steps from the abyss-viewing dining room farthest from the molecule-town. Her room, with its double-tall view of the open sea, was just steps away. Probably hundreds of steps, knowing how the marketing copy oversold everything, but still.

Aino rapidly revised her opinion of this operation, and its proprietor. Valdez Underwater Resorts wasn't just an economic driver for the planet Kitt, but most likely the main economic driver. Up top, with its slashing winds and poisonous fauna, Kitt offered nothing compared to this. Cropland enough for its paltry inhabitants and the resort's tourists, but not for export. Mining difficult, manufacturing expensive due to import fees.

Even without the special events planned, Aino would have been glad to see this. She'd have to come again, and stay longer.

Where ever had those sticky people gone? Maybe waiting out the weekend at the beach hotels until the Valdes re-opened. Mid-week rates and all. Good luck to them.

As the limo dropped closer, Aino could make out the intricate gardens around the domes. Tall pale seaweedy plants crowded the spaces between the main dome and the smaller molecule, offering privacy—and probably a lot of fish. Around the front and her side of the resorts stretched tall shelves of coral and a rainbow of plant life. Giant gardens to play in.

From above, she could easily see the round tops of the promised emergency stations, dark gray cylinders set at regular intervals around the seabed at least as far out as the width of the dome itself. At the level of seabed, they would be harder to see. Coral and plant life, which may or may not be real, draped on many of them. But at at dive suit's signal—or a diver's tapping their emergency wrist band—the nearest cylinder would announce itself and stand ready.

No one died at Valdes Underwater Resort.

Unless they were meant to.

Chapter Two

S o yeah, now Frankie knew why no one wanted to transport glimmerantin beans. She could just picture that cabal of deep-space cargo haulers back at Xeri Station laughing in their weak-tea beers when they heard she'd picked up this freight.

Ten days was all it took for the three dozen bright yellow shuttle-sized crop containers to sweat out buckets of some skanky oil.

"Vacuum sealed," the manifest had read. Sure.

But the giant containers had looked as tightly sealed as all the others she'd ever hauled, and newer than most. Reinforced dull-metal edgings over standard, if sunny bright, polymer sides. Long rectangled boxes with doors at the short ends—doors with triple seals. Two meters taller than Frankie; it was always tricky even in the half-gravity at the docks to inspect the top of each container.

So yeah, she'd signed the manifest, and watched the parade of sunflower-tinted giants float themselves into the wide waist of the big bulb of her cargo hold. That cavernous space, dim with only the lights along the curved inside braces on, dwarfed even three dozen boxes. Frankie was dead-heading back to Rosings, her home station, and couldn't afford to pass up the chance to pick up a short-haul that would cover the base cost of the trip.

Or so she'd thought.

The first hint of trouble was three days in, when she woke to a reek worse than rancid wet-wool socks. Someone had left the inner cargo bay door ajar. Someone who did not have opposable thumbs.

Frankie had to put a respirator on to force herself into the hold. The shipment huddled in neat clumps of six around the outer bay door, each container tethered separately to the wall of her ship. Their bright yellow had morphed to thick, snot green.

The oil—whatever it was—wasn't coming through the doors, but leaching through the walls of the containers themselves. Nothing she could do now—besides keep the inner door shut.

She'd thought about powering up the gravity in that part of the ship. The Spear was three bulbs stacked, like a snowman, with the hold having separate controls for gravity, temperature, and air. She'd have to start the hold spinning to create the gravitational force, and had worried that the spin would unleash the reek all along the walls of the hold. It seemed localized to the containers now, so why mess with it?

Instead, the bean goo had aerosolized itself—somehow—and spread evenly through the whole of the hold.

Frankie watched it from the oval window cut into the inner cargo bay door. Relentlessly coating everything—the walls, the long gantry/ladder she used during big runs. Eventually, even the oval window.

Thank Safra she hadn't had any other cargo.

So now she stood on one of Rosing Station's secondary docks, atmosuit on with helmet down, lightly balanced in its half-grav, glaring at her outer cargo bay door. She sure as Safra wasn't going to open the door from the inside.

"So, maybe a little problem," she said to Rosings' assistant cargo chief, standing next to her.

In the bright artificial light at the far end of this dingy too-thin metal pier jutting away from the central hub of the station, Assistant Chief Saleh's shadow stretched large as a mountain. Weird that he was even here, what with the port so noisy with freighters, all with much bigger cargo than hers. Frankie had expected one of the servos to handle the transaction.

"No time like the present," he said. In the half-gravity, the tips of his locs lifted off his green-atmosuited shoulders, giving his stern wide face a dash of whimsy. Frankie would never dare tell him that.

Right. She spun the two main latches on the cargo bay door by hand, powering on her gravity boots for support. Did the spindles feel sticky? No way those blasted beans could soak the door. Right?

The door lifted open from the bottom like a hinge.

Now the reek had texture, and force. Frankie swayed as if the smell had slapped her. She clamped her mouth shut, trying to keep foul stench out. Even Saleh wobbled a bit.

"Don't know what you expected," he said. He float-hopped away from the door, his grav-boots clamping down nearly a meter away. Frankie pushed away, too, getting more space between herself and the gunky self-propelled cargo containers slowly parading out of her ship.

Salah pressed a spot on the tablet in his hand. A rumble like a giant's snore started, and then air began to blast past them. The wind swept the reek toward the port's main outer entry. The entry, protected by a force shield, would keep the air in, but maybe not the reek.

"Never seen a shipment that didn't come in all coated in the gunk," he continued.

"Super," she said. Extra cleanup was going to suck out all the measly profit from this run. "Do I need to wrap them in something before you take shipment?" That would set her back even more. If it even worked.

"Nah," Salah said. "We always put them in the old water tank, over on the underside."

"Must smell fantastic." Frankie wrinkled her nose, but it didn't help. Back on Xeri Station, the cargo had smelled like, well, beans. Nothing much. Now she couldn't imagine anyone wanting to come near them. These beans were supposedly super tasty. What did chefs do about the reek?

"These are actually the freshest I've seen in awhile," Salah said. "And you're lucky it stuck to the packaging. Not onto all your surfaces." He peered into the hold. "Much."

Now she knew what was coming.

"Don't tell me. You know a guy can clean it up in no time."

"Brother-in-law," Sala said. "Good at mopping up." He snorted. "Just about all he's good at."

Frankie didn't say anything about that, either. She had no experience with brothers-in-law, and her experience with brothers had ended when she was eight. But she was not going down that trail of thought today.

"You want, I can call him for you," Salah said. "Get you to the top of the list."

Frankie wiped hopefully imaginary gunk off her hand and onto the back of the knee of her second-best atmosuit. "Sounds good," she said. Always good to be friendly with the station deputies. They did all the work. "Not sure when I'm headed out, yet."

Salah's wise brown eyes gave her a long look.

He wouldn't see anything she didn't want him to see.

Rosing Station was the home base for Systems Analysis Incorporated, a very-private concern that performed gray-area services for deserving clients. No one was supposed to know that Frankie worked for them. She really was a small-time hauler of cargo. But with no fixed routes, thanks to the Skoll mafia's hold on shipping, she was free to take whatever loads would get her closest to her next real assignment.

Which she did not have, yet. Not that she was worried. Not at all.

"Where's your ratty sidekick?" Salah's attention had turned back to the inside of the cargo hold.

"Hiding. I think the smell turned her stomach." How that smell had tracked its way into their living space had been a heated topic of conversation between them. With all the talking on Frankie's side.

Spike was a cat.

In public.

In fact, Spike was a cyvlossic, with a synthetically enhanced smarter-than-thou mind in the body of an oversized, scruffier-than-respectable feline. Spike had worked for SystA for years, and had recruited Frankie.

Frankie wasn't exactly sure why Spike was still with her. Hard to recruit new folks when you were spending all your time with the old ones. Then again, every assignment they'd done so far had needed the both of them, so Frankie wasn't about to complain.

Except about leaving cargo-bay doors ajar.

As the last container hummed itself through the hatch, Salah held out his tablet for Frankie to sign.

"Don't go out to the float-park," he said. He waved toward the space behind her. "Go to yellow dock, down by there. Garth's pilot license was...recalled. He has to use the docks to get to your ship. Safer for the cleaning materials, anyway."

Frankie took a deep breath of the now only metal-sharp air of the dock. Then she stepped back into her ship and reached for the door's controls.

"Thanks, Salah. You're a lifesaver," she said. She pressed the button to lever the door closed and got out of the way.

"My pleasure. And say hi to Bruce for me."

Bruce was SystA's on-station manager.

"Such a cutie, that one." Salah winked at her. "So shy."

The door clanked shut.

So much for secrecy.

Chapter Three

Supper at Valdes Underwater Resort during an Elysium Weekend was a quiet affair. The thirteen people spread out in the exclusive dining room when Aino Miller strode in didn't take up one-sixth of the space.

Mostly singles but two couples, each had a private window view. Slight indentations in the plush, sound-dampening grassy-mossy carpet suggested that a second table at each window panel had been removed, giving diners even more privacy.

The window panels, five meters wide at the floor, tapered slowly past the beige-linen-draped tables up to nearly the center of the domed room. Half the room was glass—or rather triple-reinforced acrylic-laced glassene. The merest suggestion of seams between the panels actually contained flexible, reinforced nano-mesh tendons, flexible enough to hold firm in the event of either an earthquake or a water breach.

Aino did not need to interact with the beautiful human, also dressed in burgundy, who led her to her table. They pulled out the old-fashioned upright padded chair the perfect height for her, saw her seated comfortably, and left.

The courses were chef's choice, based on a long list of preferences Aino had filled out beforehand. She thought she could smell some kind of red meat dish coming from the table behind her, but she knew none would be coming for her. Which meant her wine would be a white varietal, her favorite.

The server silently placed a chilled glass of bitingly dry white on her table in less than a minute. In the golden half-light of the dining room, the glass, with its clear stem and the pale white liquid it held, looked so gorgeous set against the otherwise untouched ecru tablecloth. Minimalist perfection. Aino almost didn't want to break the display by actually picking up and drinking the wine.

Almost.

Glass in hand, its stem cold between her fingers, she leaned against the tall back of her chair and gazed out her window. Spotlights on tall poles a good distance away from the buildings—and right at the edge of that drop-off to the left—spread a diffuse grayish light through the nearby waters. Behind the lights crashed the heavy darkness of undersea.

In the middle distance, schools of iridescent fish scampered through undulating fields of seaweeds and short channels of blond coral. Orange, blue, silver with stripes of gold flitted by. Just below her scuttled two of those foot-sized ruddy creepy-crawlies, crablike animals with four pincers.

But her gaze kept being drawn to that pit-dark abyss beyond the lights. She had to squint, but was pleased she could discern the shapes of chubby groupers, two furry rosicants, a pygmy shark. No color on these monsters—anything coming from below looked gray-dark, thick, sinister. Next meal, she would ask to sit on that side, so she could get a better look.

Savoring her seaweed gazpacho starter course, Aino coolly

studied the other patrons. Like her, most were contemplating the remarkable variety of life outside. Like her, almost all were in their late middle years, with a few very old indeed. Only one nervous looking woman looked to be in her twenties. What did she have to be nervous about? It was only Friday night.

Aino did not recognize any of her fellow travelers. She'd thought she might, but it didn't matter anyway.

What happened at Valdez Underwater Resort stayed here and only here, reinforced by the stunningly well-written nondisclosure forms they'd all had to sign. Not to mention the rule that outside-the-body communication devices must remain in the guest rooms at all times. No selfies.

She already liked it here. Everything in order. Rules enforced. Nobody slipping through the cracks, nobody sliding through on a technicality or an idiot jury.

Aino returned her attention to the panorama outside her window. A manta ray glided by, its wings hypnotic. As it disappeared into the inky blackness of the trench, the server returned with her next course: blackened pygmy shark.

Chapter Four

"The assistant dock chief knows I work for you."

Bruce, smaller than life on her apartment's vid screen, did not bat an eyelash.

"Saleh?" he said. "Fool. Told me to get rid of the sideburns." He ran a hand down the side of his face, half-hidden under a mighty tuft of wiry black hair on each side. No gray in any of it, though Frankie would swear the man was twice as old as her. Settled into a comfortably crackled fake leather chair behind a desk so old-fashioned it must have been printed special to order, Bruce shook his head.

"But he told me he didn't like my new, shorter hair, either," Frankie said. She was trying a very close-cropped style. The float-around, get-into-your-eyes look was so over, and she was tired of always dyeing her hair as well. With it this short, in its natural bronze-brown, she could pass for ten years younger. Plus, she looked nothing like the famous picture from long ago. The one that had made her famous, unwillingly, across the Cooperative Realm.

She matched Bruce's pose in the shorter, stiffer chair in front of the narrow table holding her vid screen in this tiny capsule of an apartment on station. She should upgrade. Get a room she could actually walk around in.

Housing was plentiful here now that the war on this side of the sector was allegedly over. Most of the military types had jumped over to Xeri Station and beyond. This last trip, Frankie hadn't been able to find a room on Xeri. Didn't need one anyway, to pick up a cargo.

But it would have been nice.

She and Bruce had never met in person. She had her suspicions that he wasn't even on-station, but if Saleh knew him it must be true.

Her stomach growled, anticipating lunch.

"So," she said when Bruce didn't respond. "Got something for me?"

"For you both." He reached out, using the air in front of him for his keyboard. "Where's your better half?"

"Wandering, like always," Frankie was in the middle of saying when Spike hopped into her screen's view. The cyvlossic ricocheted, catlike, from the floor to the armrest of Bruce's chair to the top of his desk. Bruce winced, startled, but didn't flinch. Sitting in front of the camera, Spike blocked all but the shiny sweep of Bruce's forehead.

Question answered.

"Wait! Spike gets to see you in person?"

Spike didn't even turn to look at her.

"She's the senior on your team," Bruce said.

"What team? I must be done with probation by now."

"Systems thinks you do better as a team." Bruce might have shrugged, but it was hidden behind sworls of rat-tufted gray-and-cream fur. "You gonna argue with success?"

Well. That explained that.

Frankie shrugged, ignoring the pang in her belly at the sound of the ping. Her leftover miso soup had finished rewarming.

"Grab your lunch," Bruce said, ignoring her shrug if he could even see it. "This is going to take a while."

The video Bruce played for Frankie was poor quality. The image shook as if it had been recorded in secret. It took her a couple of seconds to figure out what she was seeing.

The camera operator was walking through a large empty room, set up like a mid-range planet-based restaurant dining room. Circle tables, with pretty, un-bolted-down chairs tucked under them, bumping into their white tablecloths.

"We'll watch it through, and then talk," Bruce said. "There's no sound."

Now the view was out one of the tall windows at the edge of the room, into deep gray-blue water.

"Restaurant under water?" Frankie said.

"Deep-sea resort." Bruce said. "Chance to be one with the sea, all that."

Now she could see people outside the window, diving masks on their faces, flippers on their feet. Minnowing this way and that, wherever caught their eye.

Only some of them were in full diving suits. Most had half-suits or long swimsuits, but a couple were in those skimpy things. Bikinis.

Below them, paths of light sand were outlined by whorls and walls of coral. Mostly reds and whites, but some blues and some amazing purples. A planned garden?

Fish, clearly used to the sight of humans flopping about, zipped among and around the divers. Freddie wondered if dolphins came around, or bigger fish.

In the distance, tall, thin wood-looking posts set maybe two meters apart from one another marked some sort of boundary. There was no coral or plant growth on any part of the posts.

The bright-pink bikini person with the flowing hair was flopping around around close to the boundary. She needed more practice with her bright-pink flippers. A clearly more-experienced diver in a gray half-suit and wearing one of those overachieving wristcoms shadowed her. The water past this part of the boundary looked somehow darker. Frankie didn't know oceans, but she was pretty sure that the resort must need to add to the lighting.

She shivered. The girl must be freezing. She was so pale to begin with. And all that pressure. At least space diving didn't give you the bends. And people almost never drowned.

There must have been some signal, off screen. People stopped what they were doing and started swimming to the left and down. At the left corner of the screen, Frankie could see part of a dive-suited arm, wearing another of those shiny massive wristcoms, waving the swimmers in.

Soon all were gone, leaving only the couple by the far boundary.

The view crash-zoomed in, grainier and shakier, focusing on the two swimmers.

"From here, two minutes have been cut out," Bruce said. "Just swimming around."

The picture jerked, still on the two swimmers. but Frankie didn't see the post anymore. Must be between posts.

The bikini person turned away from looking out past the boundary to looking into the safe area. Her hair swirled behind her and to the side. She wore a clear half-mask that didn't hide her eyes. She wasn't wearing an oxygen tank. Her breathing rig was tied—tubed—to the other diver, piggybacking off one of the three tanks the other diver wore.

Really being one with the sea, this one.

Her head turned as if she were sweeping the view. Just now realizing they were all alone out there?

Her body turned to face her companion. She'd gone vertical, slowly pumping the flippers to stay upright. She pointed to the left, where the other swimmers had gone. Her companion slowly shook his head. They lifted their wrist, tapping the comm.

Did they mean it wasn't time yet? Time for what?

The girl pointed again, jamming her finger hard twice. The other diver turned to look. Their mask was dark, and they had their hood on.

The camera followed their line of sight. The wrist that had been sweeping divers in now was moving in a circle. A different signal.

Then it stopped. The hand fisted. The arm came down in a chopping motion.

The view slammed back to the couple. They were closer to each other now, the bigger diver's body blocking bikini girl from sight except for her pink flippers.

Then the diver moved to the side.

Blood bloomed black from a long clean slice across the girl's bare midriff.

She looked down, and then back to her companion. Her mouthpiece wobbled, as if she'd started talking and forgotten no air surrounded her. She clutched her middle with one arm and reached for her companion with the other.

The other diver came closer, but didn't take her hand. Instead, they put both their hands—one holding something that looked like a bloody knife—on her shoulders. And pushed.

The girl shot backwards. As she crossed the boundary, it lit up briefly, like the flash on a speed trap camera.

Now the girl's shoulders were shaking hard. She must be

starting to hyperventilate. She curled herself to get her head pointed toward the boundary and kicked her flippers hard.

Her head hit the boundary, and stopped.

Stunned, she grabbed her head with both hands. The blood from her cut flowed freely now.

She pounded on the boundary. It looked like nothing, but it did not give.

She was outside.

Her companion did not come closer to the boundary. They reached out, but not for her. They cut the air tube between them. The tube jerked away, losing air. The big diver propelled themself quickly backward. The bikini-clad girl was not getting dragged along.

She was alone.

Trails of blood circled around her, as if she were in the eye of a slow-motion watery tornado. She curled into herself, wrapping both arms around her middle.

Behind her, a shadow slowly rose from below. Bigger, and bigger.

A giant shark, mouth wider than the girl was long.

The girl didn't seem to notice. Now she was almost a ball, tucked in so tightly to herself.

The shark's mouth slowly opened.

The girl must have sensed something. Maybe the draw of the water into the monster's mouth.

She popped out of her ball, saw the shark and started to move. Jerking sideways away from the shark. But her arms and legs didn't work together, panicked. She wasn't moving fast enough.

Now she wasn't moving at all.

Frankie closed her eyes.

Chapter Five

S ome brief time later, Frankie heard Bruce clear his throat. She cracked open one eye. The video was still on. The girl was gone. Just thick blood stringing along the roil of the water. The shark's top fin, sinking back into the depths.

The view changed back to Bruce, safe in his office.

"Her name was Natalie Stone. Her death was ruled accidental, based on eyewitness testimony and another video, shot at a different angle, and edited to delete the diver's actions." He snorted. "In the other video, all you see of the diver is that last part, him swimming toward Natalie but not reaching her in time."

Frankie found she had her arms wrapped around her middle. She'd forgotten to breathe for who knew how long. Half a minute.

"Why did you show me that?" she croaked.

"Natalie was not the first. This resort appears to have a regular murder package tour." Bruce flicked his hand at her. "Sending you the details now."

Frankie shook her head. She didn't want any details. She was a cargo hauler. A data pusher. Maybe a low-key investigations assistant. She didn't even know how to shoot a gun.

"Why? I'm not a murder detective." Frankie couldn't keep her voice in its normal low register. "Tell the Cooperative."

Bruce paused. He seemed to actually look at her.

"Do you need a minute?"

"A minute!" Frankie had found her breath. "You just showed me a snuff film! No warning whatsoever! How am I supposed to feel?"

"Right, Spike." Bruce said, looking off screen. "I forgot. You're still new at this."

"At this?" Frankie's voice hit high C. "Safra's blasted comets. I'm an information drone, not some murder action hero. These people are bad."

"Relax, Frankie," Bruce said, honey in his voice.

"Fuck you."

"Right." Bruce went back to professional-stern. "We're not asking you to do anything rough. We have a line on the next girl they plan to—" He paused. "Use this way."

Frankie shivered. The happy warmth from the miso soup was gone.

"All we need you and Spike to do is get her clear. Out of their grasp. Then our people—our other people—can do the rest."

"Stop her before she gets there?"

"Ideally." Bruce said, sighing. "But we predict only a five percent success rate with that."

He rubbed down his mighty sideburn again.

"So. Frankie. Congratulations. You just won an all-expenses paid vacation at the bottom of the sea."

The air limo again enveloped Aino Miller in its velvet embrace, the soft burr of its movement a comforting hum. Slowly, the underwater resort shrank away beneath her as the vehicle began its eight-plus hour ascent to the surface.

She had to hand it to Monica Valdes and her resort staff. Aino had been the only guest at the entrance, and this the only limo. All sixteen of the weekend's guests—fifteen now—must be spaced far enough apart that each had the illusion of solitude as they contemplated their adventure.

Aino's fingers danced on the armrest, her body unable to contain the satisfaction buzzing in her veins. And why should it? She was alone, and buzzed.

Watching the setup to the attack had been just as exciting as the actual attack. The cluelessness of the girl. The moment she noticed that something was wrong. The abject panic on her face as she pounded on the invisible barrier keeping her on the wrong side of the wild ocean.

The cobalt gray of the shark, its face all teeth, floating up from the dark deep like a stage actor landing perfectly on his cue. Pausing for the girl to turn, but not so long that she could even start to flee.

The girl didn't fight, or flee. She froze. No body fat on her, she'd already started sinking when that serrated maw of a mouth latched onto her.

That part, the mauling, was less satisfying. The first part was below the level of the ledge of the abyss. Everyone in the observation room stood up, as if that would help them see over a ledge one hundred meters away. By the time the shark rose again—only a half-minute, less—the body was just meat and bone, maybe a hand intact but Aino couldn't be sure.

The girl hadn't been a girl in Aino's imagination, though. The judge had replaced the girl's body in her mind with the equally slim silhouette of Samuel DaFilono, the slipperiest character ever to come through her courtroom. Four—at least four—murders could be laid at his doorstep. Three reached prosecution, so far. And none—not one—case against him had convinced a jury.

The kid was slick as silicon.

The last time, when the jury foreperson answered "not guilty," DaFilono had the audacity to wink at Aino. At least she hadn't had to watch him saunter out of the room. Judges got to leave first.

Nothing she could do to him. Injustice made flesh.

But here, this place, offered her a safe outlet for that frustration, that aggression, forever building up. Years forced to observe the relentless parade of venality, that grotesque carnival of criminality, that paraded through her courtrooms and her with little—so little—to do that would even stem the tide

Here, she could indulge in her darkness without fear of consequence.

A message came through from the resort. There had been a tragic accident in the open-swim area. A wayward diver, out on her own past the posted time. The last guests were departing when staff noticed she was not among them. Obviously guests should not expect to be questioned about the incident, but were advised to go straight to the off-planet shuttle platform.

Aino must have been one of the last guests to leave.

Her limo pulled smoothly onto the first half-domed cul-de-sac turnoff on the side of the tunnel-road. Time to stretch and walk out the air bubbles, or however they put it.

The door opened, and Aino stepped out. She peered out at the dark water, already a shade lighter than below, even here on the first stop. She looked down, down, hoping to see the shark again, or one of its brethren. No luck.

Back the monster had gone into its crevasse.

Until next time.

Next time.

Perhaps she should make this a regular retreat.

Chapter Six

S hepherd Orbital Station creeped Frankie out.

It wasn't just the cylindrical shape of the station, with its stacked neighborhoods along the so, so long hallways. Nor the mushroom cap at one end, which held the components that kept the station aloft and yet looked like it could pop right off at a touch. It was more the absolute lack of young people.

Families who lived on-station held to a tradition of sending all their university-age kids away, to try life on planets or to further their educations. A noble goal, sure, but the utter lack of twenty-somethings and even most thirty-somethings felt like a breach in the structure of Shepherd Station's society. Not to mention the scarcity of places to flirt while you danced.

Frankie liked it better here on her Spear. She sat slouched, one foot tucked under her on the wide pilot's seat in the center of her ship's tiny bean of a control room. She took a sip of her lukewarm tea, wiggled the toes of her other foot, propped on the edge of the powered-down control-paneled table in front of her, and released the cargo hauler's controls to auto-dock.

Spike sat on the seat to her right, the seat that used to be Frankie's, the one that was closest to the entryway. Not that Frankie still begrudged her about it, or anything. Spike had a paw caught behind her own ear, stuck in an unusually egregious tuft of her disreputable pelt. Frankie pretended not to notice as her colleague wrestled with her own piebald fur to dislodge her paw.

Instead, she focused on catching up on local news on one floating screen while she kept an eye on the Spear's outside cameras on a second and third screen. The ship gracefully eased into her designated berth, and extended the docking ramp to the hopefully air-supplied dock.

A small servo rolled toward the ramp. Behind it floated a small cargo container.

Frankie chanced a glance at Spike. The cyvlossic still had a paw up, but at least it was free. Its knifelike claws were fully out, and Spike seemed to be glaring at them.

"Cargo incoming," Frankie said. "Order anything?"

With the slightest tilt of her wide, dark head, Spike transferred her glare to Frankie.

"Right," Frankie said. She tapped the incoming message from the servo, accepted the container and its controls, and ordered the Spear to allow it in to float on up to them.

It was a package from Bruce. Frankie had it float behind and between their chairs and then gently come to rest on the floor.

She looked a question at Spike, who shrugged, dropping her paw to the seat. Why would their boss need to send anything after them? Why didn't he give it to them six days ago, back at Rosings? Frankie already knew how it got here so fast. The Spear had been at mid-speed. No reason to get here early, when the tourist they were looking for wouldn't get here until days before the big killer weekend.

The container, which only looked like a standard gray beat-up small-cargo box, was triple-thick and double-locked. Frankie managed the first lock with her basic ID, but she had to take a minute to scare up which secret-code key they were using this week to solve the second lock.

Inside, on top of what looked like clothing and real pieces of cotton-style paper, were new instructions in the form of an old-fashioned chip.

"Seriously?" Frankie said. She hauled herself upright and reached for the chip. Where was that chip reader, anyway?

Spike jumped up onto the pilot's board. She padded over to the far end and sat down, pointedly.

Right. The chip slot was over there.

Frankie clicked open the tiny, stiff case holding the chip, and then slid it across the board to Spike. The cyvlossic pried the chip out of the case with its freakishly flexible toe beans, and slid it into the card reader. The chip reader click-clonked, reminding Frankie of her school days sneaking bad movies and worse love poetry past her guardians via chips like these.

A hologram of the top half of Bruce popped up between them. Frankie's boots hit the ground and she was almost out of her chair before she realized it was an image. Spike tilted her head, looking at Frankie like she was an especially dumb bug.

"Greetings, team," Bruce said. "We're having a bit of a virus here in our comm systems. Not sure it's intentional but we're treating it as if it is. So, we're going old-school: one-way communication."

Bruce's holo looked to the left, towards Frankie.

"Yeah, Spike, I heard you laughing. You told us so. Came in via the secondary switcher." Bruce shrugged. "When you're right, you're right."

Spike strutted across the board so she'd be in holo-Bruce's line of sight, and preened.

"Anyway," Bruce said. "Here's the deal. We found the girl. Aimee Sansom, from Central System. Child of a very successful corporate executive, just like all the others."

Frankie eased back into her chair. She called up the text and image files also stored on the chip and started skimming through them.

Aimee Sansom looked like half the femme Central City socialites Frankie had ever met. Pasty pale, blond, big blue eyes enhanced to look even bigger. Hair long enough to pull into a horsetail. Too thin. Way too thin.

Her life also read like a cliché. Good schools, fair grades, expensive hobbies. No major health issues. Two older siblings. Some do-gooding activities, but no more than required and none that actually required talking to the downtrodden folks she was allegedly trying to help.

Bruce was still talking.

"Unfortunately, this Aimee is not due into Shepherd until an hour or so before her scheduled shuttle departure down to Kitt. Cutting it close. Plus, she's going down a day earlier than the rest of the guests. Unexpected." Irritating, Bruce's tone implied. "You'll need to catch her at the terminal, after she gets off the transport and before she gets on the shuttle."

Frankie rolled her eyes. Sometimes Bruce could be Mr. Exposition. This time, though, he was probably overcompensating for not being able to see them. Spike bumped Frankie's elbow, a warm push.

"I know you're not a master of spy craft, but with this tight time frame, we're changing the brief." Bruce waved toward the doorway. "In the box, you'll find a small tin holding a strip of of tracking chips. They look like pale skin tags, with adhesive on one side. We want you to adhere one to Sansom's skin—probably her hairline in back—in the waiting area. Or get Spike to bite her."

32

Spike hissed. She stood on her haunches and batted a paw through holo-Bruce's neck.

Frankie leaned over the box and picked up the tin. The tags were tiny. But what happened to the plan to prevent the girl from getting on the shuttle in the first place?

"Now that we know more about her, we don't think you can persuade her fast enough that she is in danger," holo-Bruce said. Because Frankie didn't look like a socialite? "Especially not without scaring her away from you, too." Bruce fingered his chin where the sideburns met it. "If you can't, but you get the tag on her, then the rescue team can sweep in and get her off the shuttle. If not there, then we'll know where she is on Kitt."

Frankie leaned back into the chair. Could she really do this? She looked at Spike, the real spy expert.

Spike growled low at her. At least she didn't swipe at her neck.

"Fine," Frankie said out loud. Holo-Bruce seemed to hear her.

"With all this, we still predict eighty percent chance of success," he said. "Not good enough. So, here's Plan B: Spike and Frankie go on vacation."

Ha ha. Their last vacation had gone off the rails when they had had to rescue another cyvlossic, Sunshine, from a bad situation. Not much rest and relaxation there.

Holo-Bruce sighed. Frankie was surprised that he hadn't cut that out, or had his assistant do it. Although the assistant was probably deep in the search for whatever that comms virus was.

"In the box you'll find some sample clothing, and patterns for you to print up more. Check out your dossiers. You're getting upgraded. Socialites." The way Bruce said it made it sound like parasites. "You'll want to be these characters when you meet up with Sansom. Plausible deniability, you know."

Frankie did not know, but at the first touch of the fabric, she absolutely did not care.

Velvet! She pulled out a gorgeous black-navy jacket. And, under that, the softest silk in soft sunset rose. Two things impossible for even her new top-of-the-line printer to recreate.

She slipped the shiny blue jacket on over her Vapid Trances t-shirt; it fit perfectly. Cut bolero style, the front was open and the bottom seam hit just below her ribs. Perfect with a simple sheath or a complicated blouse. Perfect against her warm sienna skin.

Under that were fancy-looking flippers and what looked like a complete underwater breathing apparatus.

Frankie left those where they lay. But she scooped up a small bottle of perfume. She held it to her inner wrist, and pressed the plunger only halfway.

The entire small room exploded in jasmine. The flowery, almost honey-like scent overwhelmed the air scrubbers, turning the tiny room into a summer's day.

Spike sneezed. And sneezed again. Luckily, the screen the cyvlossic had pulled up to look at her own documents was not physical. The sneeze droplets sailed right through.

And landed on the pilot's console.

Not looking at the mess, Frankie turned back to the data on her screen, and pulled up the file marked IDs.

Evelyn Crowe, the shy heiress to a healthy-drinks empire. Not seen much in public, so no one could know much about her except she had enough credits and sway to qualify for attendance at a very private resort weekend.

"Precious," Spike hissed. The cyvlossic's implanted voice box had been damaged at some point, and Spike had never had it repaired. Frankie had asked Sunshine about it during the rescue—Sunshine's voice was gorgeous—and Sunshine had told her to ask Spike. Frankie hadn't worked up the nerve yet to ask.

"You're cover is precious?" Frankie said. She looked over at Spike's screen.

Worse than that. Spike's fake name was Precious.

Frankie looked at her colleague, whose resting face was "don't touch me." Whose long fur did not behave. Who slunk and sneered. And sneezed.

"Kind of a stretch for you, then?"

Spike growled again, sounding even less friendly.

Frankie gave her colleague some space. She turned back to her own screen.

Not only did Evelyn Crowe have a dossier, but she had a media trail as well. How had SystA done this so fast? The popular reporting and rare personal posts painted Frankie's fake self as a mysterious and powerful figure with tragic undertones. The need for a comfort animal added an extra layer of intrigue.

"Well, at least we are supposed to be eccentric and rude," Frankie muttered, her eyes narrowing as she focused on the images and posts.

Most surprising, Evelyn and Precious had already done an interview with the owner of Valdes Underwater Resorts. Frankie pointed at the media file, and looked at Spike.

"Hit it," Spike growled. Frankie activated the recording.

The uncanny resemblance of the actors to Frankie and Spike sent a chill down Frankie's spine. Spike's friend, Sunshine, dyed to match Spike's coloring, did an adequate job of mimicking her. Except for the perfect fur and Sunshine's expression of adoration toward her comfort person.

The fake-Frankie playing Evelyn was equally polished. Where ever had they found this person? Did other people think she was really so brown and square?

Luckily, Frankie already could conjure up the manners befitting an Evelyn Crowe, thanks to a tough headmistress during her teenage years. And the vocabulary, thanks to the same headmistress. But this recorded version of Evelyn had a voice nothing like hers. She'd have to pitch her voice much higher than usual.

The interviewer—Monica Valdes herself, owner of the resort—was in another world altogether. Even in a deceptively simple looking black turtleneck and slacks, she seamlessly blended classic elegance and cutting-edge style. Pale skin, almost translucent blue, was surely a result of genetic modifications that allowed her to thrive for long stretches in her underwater environment. Shimmering silver hair was styled perfectly to frame her angular features. Her eyes, a startling violet, were probably enhanced to help her absorb light in the depths of the ocean.

Despite her otherworldly appearance—startling, in a system where enhancements are frowned upon—she exuded warmth and charm. Frankie relaxed, watching her. And then tensed, realizing what a formidable opponent she would be.

If anyone knew anything about these killings it would be Valdes, the resort's sole owner.

Suddenly, the whole idea seemed impossible. Frankie took perverse pride in telling the truth, a trait that had not endeared her to the socialites of Central City. Could she lie so much now, well enough to fool a pro like Monica Valdes?

Not a chance.

"I don't want to do this," Frankie said. She looked at Spike. "I don't want you to have to do this."

They needed to catch Aimee at the gate. Never go near the planet, the ocean, the resort. Get the girl, and let SystA's pros work the real investigation.

Tomorrow.

Chapter Seven

To practice acting as Evelyn and Precious before their big performance at the passenger terminal, Frankie and Spike decided to forgo the tram and walk. Or rather, stroll.

It wouldn't take too much longer. It was a half-hour walk, and their target, Aimee Samson, wasn't due to arrive for an hour. Plus, with only a small detour, they could spend the bulk of the time in what the station called its "opulent collective oasis."

So okay, the park really was gorgeous. Even in a tricky beaded wrap dress and matching espadrilles in the latest CapCity style, Frankie felt outclassed. And Spike, well. After submitting to Frankie's over-gentle until finally over-aggressive brushing, Spike's fur was all going the same direction, at least.

The park was a symphony of color, texture, and scent. Each flower and plant had been precisely placed to create a harmonious balance, at least for Capital City human tastes.

Real trees of several sorts spread their branches above them, reaching toward the banks of filtered sun lights five stories above.

Under the trees dozed sizable beds of flowers and plants in vibrant palettes of pink, blue, yellow, green, rainbow. The beds were set apart from wide sandy looking walkways by 10 cm berms in the same sandy material. Even the clover lawn and several short-grass lawns were set into beds.

The air was tart with the smell of freshly-cut grass, crowding out the more delicate fragrances of the flowers. Some water feature burbled nearby, but Frankie didn't want to leave the path between all the flower beds to look for it. They didn't have forever, after all.

Because the fancy dress didn't allow her to bend too far forward, Frankie squatted gracefully at the side of a bed of perfect violets. Now she could taste the purple.

The gentle rustle of leaves and the distant chirping of birds—could they be real?—almost completely masked the fact that busy tram lines, shopping districts, and the bustle of a mid-size city were just a five-minute walk away.

Here, the walkers were few. Most people on-station worked the day shift, especially the times when the shuttles and cargo arrived. They had the park nearly to themselves, except for an older couple walking along a parallel path and a dozen small children, off in the distance on one of the lawns, playing some sort of hopping game.

Spike sniffed at the violets dismissively. Her eyes were on the trees with the low branches two beds away.

"We don't have time to chase birds," Frankie said teasingly.

Spike looked at her as if she were a really stupid bug.

"You're right, sorry, bad joke," she said. Frankie tried to stand all in one graceful movement, arms at her sides, but her hands had to lift to get the legs in proper order. It had been years since she'd needed to don the full CapCity persona. The fit was as awkward as ever, but at least she didn't have to chit-chat with anyone. Or remember the impossible knot of alliances and estrangements that tied the Top Five Hundred together.

Spike stuck close to her, very like a companion animal, as they strolled toward the bed of trees. But Frankie could feel the vibration of the cyvlossic's excitement at the idea of a hunt. They would have to return here afterward, so Spike could run around. So Frankie could run around, once she got back into her favorite soft, obviously cheap-printer-made togs.

They had made it past the taller trees with no incident when Frankie spied a tea shop in the distance. And Spike made a new enemy.

"Stop!" someone shouted behind them. She was dressed in Shepherd security's dull brown jacket over even duller tan top and pants. Red-cheeked and winded, she wiped her brow.

"Finally caught up to you," she said. "Saw you at the peonies. Didn't you hear me calling?"

Frankie hadn't heard anything. The tall woman's voice was reedy, and Frankie's ears had been tuned to a different range.

"My apologies, officer."

"Deputy. Took me this long to catch up." The deputy leaned back, hands on her lower back, and took in a deep breath. "Anyway," she said on the exhale. "You have to leave."

"Pardon me?" Frankie used the tone she'd heard from so many of her instructors in the past. Imperious, affronted.

"Yes, sorry. Well, no. You're breaking the law."

"By strolling?" Frankie pulled her spine up, trying to look down her nose at the deputy. Of course, she had to lean back to do it, as the deputy had half a meter on her in height.

"Imported animals are strictly prohibited on the station," the deputy stated firmly, her hand resting on the what looked like a tiny electroshock baton at her side. Spike glommed onto Frankie's ankles, hiding behind her.

"Precious isn't an animal," Frankie said, remembering Spike's new name in the nick of time. "She's my comfort animal."

That stopped the deputy, for half a second.

"You know, you just said animal twice?" The deputy pulled out the baton. It took all the imaginary force of her old teacher, Proctor Lizbet, to keep Frankie from taking a step back.

The deputy looked at Spike, looked at her baton, and then looked at Frankie down and up.

A buzzing started a meter above Frankie's head, and then draped itself around her.

A cylindrical force field.

Spike head-butted it, and yelped in pain or pique. The cyvlossic sat on the ground, hard.

Seriously? Straight to a cage? Not even a short stop at hand-cuffs or—Safra forbid—a short discussion first?

This couldn't be happening. Frankie's face started to burn.

They had to get to the boarding area.

They had to catch up with Aimee Samson.

Frankie's fingers clenched the folds of her dress in bewildered frustration. The top-quality fabric neatly sliced her fingers in dozens of places.

Spike head-butted Frankie. Frankie, jolted out of the beginnings of a panic loop, looked down at her. Spike held up a paw straight, and then curled it in toward her face. And held it there, staring at Frankie.

Right, duh. She wasn't completely helpless. Frankie checked her wristcom, trying to decide whether to call Bruce or text his assistant first.

The comm was dead. Dampened by whatever this force field was.

Frankie stupidly stared at the comm, and then equally stupidly stared at Spike.

Spike very carefully lifted her wrist and mocked a bite on its edge.

Right. The SOS button. An "all hands, please help" siren that only SystA people could hear.

Frankie dropped to Spike's height, and hugged her. After all, Precious was supposed to be her support animal, right?

Spike only startled a little bit. She even started a soft purr that somehow also sounded grudging.

"That button's one-use only," Frankie said to the back of Spike's neck. "Emergency."

Spike said nothing. The purring stopped.

Right. Of course. Emergency.

Frankie twisted the comm on her wrist until she could get to its back plate. Using one of Evelyn's newly honed fingernails, she flicked an inset latch, popping open a compartment encasing a single black pinhead of a button.

As she pressed it, a sweep of honey brown hair fell across her forehead. Frankie jumped straight up, startled.

It was her own hair, now in Evelyn's shade.

She had to calm down. She wasn't a spy.

She was a spy today.

She was a bad spy today.

Counting her inhale, counting her exhale, Frankie scanned the park. People were staring at them, or trying not to stare at them. The deputy was staring at her baton/comm thingie. Probably sending for a hazmat team.

Frankie's face started to get hot.

No. This wasn't going to happen.

It wouldn't be happening, to Evelyn Crowe, powerful heiress to the BlueEnergy beverage empire.

She had to be Evelyn Crowe.

"Abominable girl!" Frankie said, pitching her voice down and low. The deputy startled, and looked up from her device. "Of course I have my documents in order. But you—" she waved her wristcommed hand at the deputy. "You are keeping me from showing you the truth. It's in my documents."

Frankie glanced around. The older couple had stopped, and were listening. A trio of new people who looked like siblings was coming up to them on the path. She raised her voice.

"You didn't even look at my documents! You didn't even ask to see them!"

The siblings looked at one another. They started to walk faster toward Frankie.

The deputy held up her empty hands, baton dangling by a strap at her wrist. At the same moment, the air around Frankie sizzled again. She stretched her hand out.

The barrier was gone.

"Finally!" she said to the deputy, whose eyes registered confusion and a shade of worry. "Now here." Frankie popped up a screen from her comm. "Here is the passport for my little Precious." She would not look at how Spike reacted to that endearment. "And here is her medical record. And mine as well. And now, if you please, where is the office where I can lodge my complaint?"

"Problem?" A short, buxom stranger in similar garb to the deputy stepped out from the pod of trees behind the deputy. As soon as she saw the stranger, the deputy stiffened.

"Stray cat, sir," she said.

"Precious is *not* a cat," Frankie said. "Are you the deputy's superior?"

"Could say so," said the stranger, whose hair was braided close to her head like a net. "Gem Strand, head of base security." They looked out at the lawn beside them. "Taking a nice, relaxing walk in the park."

"Chief," the deputy said. "It's not what you think."

Gem side-eyed the deputy. "Why don't you tell me all about it. In my office. When you come off-shift."

Then the chief turned the whole of her attention on Frankie. "If you'll come with me, we can get this all sorted." They gestured in the right direction, toward the exit closest to the shuttle departure area.

The chief had a stride to match a sprinter's. Frankie had to jump to catch up.

"Oh, thank you so much," she started to gush, in her best Evelyn voice. "I'm so glad you came along."

"You pushed the button, didn't you?" The chief didn't even look at her, just kept scanning the environment.

"What?" Frankie caught on a beat later. "You're SystA?" she whispered.

Gem wasn't looking at her, and their steps were getting even faster. "Stop at the tea kiosk."

"Brilliant, yes. Warm matcha, does a body good." Especially when the adrenaline crash kicked in, any time now.

As Frankie was about to step up to the automated kiosk and order, Gem stopped her. The chief held out their hand.

"Give me the comm," they muttered. Frankie unstrapped it and set it into Gem's palm. "Go get your tea."

Frankie joined Gem at one of the tall round standing tables scattered non-randomly around the kiosk. Spike flung herself down on Frankie's feet. No one else was around.

The wristcom lay upside down on a piece of fabric, back wide open. The entire button housing was out, and Gem was using black tweezers to set a new one in. The whole operation was complete before Frankie had taken her third sip of tea.

Gem closed the back, inspected the front, and handed it back to Frankie.

"Most of us never use that button," they said.

Frankie stamped down the shame and frustration that threatened to show on her face.

"Most of you are professionals," she said.

"Exactly," Gem said.

"I didn't ask for this job," Frankie said. "You want it?"

Gem rolled their eyes, a muddy shade of green set into pinkish sclera. "I'm not the princess." They glanced at their own wristcom. "Just get the girl, so we don't have to. Her transport's disembarking now."

Startled, Frankie checked the time.

Blast it all. The deep-transit ship was a half-hour early.

"Must've got an earlier slip," Gem said. "Calling you an autotrike now." They pointed. "Over there."

As Frankie clipped the lid onto her tea and disentangled her feet from her colleague, she couldn't decide whether to thank Gem or snarl at them. In the end, she just started to run.

The autotrike got them to the departure area in less than ten minutes. It took another five to get them to down-planet departures.

They had to dodge through an absolute circus of humanity waiting on shuttles at the first three gates. The beaches must be great on Kitt, because everyone was dressed for sun and surf, with boards, fins, and loud, loud kids.

But when they reached the gate they wanted, 4-B, the area was empty.

Frankie ran to the gate's automated kiosk. The shuttle's gate must have gotten switched. They'd probably run right past Aimee Sansom.

Or not.

A knot of worry twisted in her chest.

Shuttle departed, the kiosk reported.

Safra's butt.

"Why?" Frankie wailed aloud.

"Every ticketed had arrived and boarded. It is the ShuttleBye way to ensure everyone's happy travels. We were glad to send them off to arrive at their destinations with time to spare."

"Safra's tits."

"We regret your dismay," the kiosk answered. "Perhaps next time you might consider obtaining a ticket in advance."

Total fail. Had she sentenced this girl to death, through her bungling?

Frankie sank on her shins. She wrapped her arms around Spike's neck again. This time, the purring that started up felt comforting.

She would not get this girl killed.

She absolutely would not.

Even if it meant SystA's whole team would have to go the bottom of the ocean.

Where the odds of their success were even less.

Chapter Eight

E ven after an hour in an air limo, gazing out the clear tunnel ceiling at the stunning ocean flora and fauna flowing above and around them as they descended, Frankie still wasn't ready for the main entry dome of Valdes Underwater Resort.

From the first step, onto a composite floor that somehow suggested soft sand, she felt wrapped in a blanket of aquatic serenity. The transparent wall that made up the back half of the dome offered a panoramic view of the dark, dark water outside. Strong white spotlights highlighted slices of vibrant animal life, diverse coral reefs, and strange geological formations. Somehow, the angle of the window did not include the many other domes and buildings.

Frankie was halfway across the wide entry dome before she began to see the tops of the other sections of the resort through the window. At this height, the hexagons, domes, and connecting tubes and pods looked as if they were, if not natural parts of the sea bed, at least parts that had been there a good long time. All of the pieces were arrayed harmoniously amid the plant and coral life.

Clean air drifted past Frankie's skin, a soft hum the only suggestion of the advanced systems powering the slightest of breezes. Overlaying the hum wasn't music, exactly, but a sound-scape of what must be actual melodies of the sea.

She breathed deep, tasting a delicate blend of salt and some kind of tropical fruit or flower. The colors of the surface water were reflected in the interior design of the resort, with hues of azure, turquoise, and aquamarine dominating the palette. The darker tones of this lower depth spiced the sweetness of the palette with slashes of red, black and stark white.

Beside her, Spike plodded along, her lumpy form and clearly shedding fur a stark contrast to the clean, sleek lines of the sloping walls and seating area. Spike had taken some cyvlossic-approved med in the limo, but it didn't seem to be helping much. Frankie felt as out of place as Spike looked, though they were both impec-cably groomed.

Nonsense. She was Evelyn Crowe, and she was wearing a gorgeous two-piece pantsuit that cost half of what Frankie Styles made in a year. Evelyn was made for this place.

Without stopping, Frankie passed what must be the welcome desk. No one was standing beside the wave-shaped waist-high wedge of white sandstone. Nobody seemed to be anywhere near.

Must be part of the VIP package: A quiet moment alone to absorb this new world.

As she reached the window, a flat circle of a fish drew near. Shiny orange as it swam out of the spotlight's glare, the fish nearly disappeared in the bare inches of space before the next swath of light. Now it looked only a hand's breadth away from Spike's face. Spike, who had her eyes closed. The descent had seriously thrown off Spike's vibe.

Frankie knelt at the window. With one hand, she stroked Spike's rough neck. With the other, she reached out, toward the orange-again fish. Just as she was about to touch the surface of the window, a shadow fell over her, Spike, and that orange pancake of a fish.

The fish didn't even pause, just darted away like a crooked arrow. Frankie dropped her hand and looked farther up the window. At the reflection of a beautiful woman.

Monica Valdes herself, all elegance and sophistication. Her pale, translucent blue skin glowed under the soft lighting almost as much as her liquid-metallic caftan. Her shimmering silver hair was styled in a sleek, asymmetrical bob that framed her angular features.

Her feet were bare.

Frankie lurched to a stand, feeling already at a disadvantage. Spike sagged against Frankie's pant leg.

Violet eyes, enhanced for water vision by nano-implants, fixed upon Frankie and Spike with a mix of warmth and what felt like suspicion.

"Welcome to Valdes Underwater Resort," Valdes said, her voice a melodic whisper that seemed to fill the space. "Ms. Crowe. It's a pleasure to meet you in person." She extended a hand.

Frankie grasped the hand, feeling the cool sleekness of Valdes's genetically modified skin. Even the resort owner's lungs had been altered to allow her to thrive in this, her chosen environment. Pretty ballsy, in a system where mods weren't exactly popular.

Someone who would go to such effort to make a go of her business didn't seem the sort who would endanger it all by repeatedly sending young women to their deaths. But surely nothing happened here that this woman did not completely control. Monica Valdez was a puzzle.

Frankie cleared her throat, preparing to push her voice into Evelyn's register.

"Beautiful place," she said. Or, rather, squeaked. Her hand went to her throat in surprise.

Valdes's eyes crinkled at the corners. "Your vocal cords can't get used to this much pressure. We have to add helium to the oxygen mixture to help people breathe. You'll find nearly everyone this weekend will sound like they've been huffing balloons." She said this in a beautiful alto voice, of course.

"Our goal here is to bathe our guests in tranquility and wonder. This is a place where the boundaries between the natural and artificial world blur, where technology and nature coexist in harmony." She gestured toward the window. "A place that invites you to explore, to relax, and to immerse yourself in the beauty of the underwater world."

Her gaze lingered on Spike, a slight suggestion of a frown at the corners of her mouth. "I trust your journey was pleasant?"

"It was." Frankie took another look at Spike, whose slight sway kept bumping into Frankie's shin. "But my Precious, here, seems a bit unsettled by the change in environment."

Spike let out a low, guttural sound, her simulated voice not affected by the underwater pressure but not really forming a word, either. Luckily. Spike's eyes seemed to lose focus for a moment.

"Ah," Valdes said. "Yes. A small number of guests experience something akin to seasickness during their first few hours here."

"She took something for it in the limo," Frankie offered. "But it wasn't enough."

"Time will heal." Valdes gestured towards the nearest seating area, another sandstone-looking wave farther along the window. "Usually I have guests rest here while I explain the protocols for the weekend. But I can just as easily explain on our way to your room. Faster for the kitty to get the rest she needs."

It was a worrisome measure of how sick Spike must feel that the cyvlossic had nothing to say about this piece of unintended slander.

Valdes directed Frankie and Spike to a vertical oval opening at the left side of the bank of windows. Stepping through the opening, they found themselves in a clear cylindrical passageway.

"All our dome villages and facilities are connected by these pressurized cylindrical passages, allowing for easy and safe movement," Valdes said. "Each is equipped with airtight seals and bulkheads to ensure the integrity of the resort. Each opens and closes the same way, like this." She demonstrated by touching a panel next to the door. "Below each panel, here, is a cabinet you can open by pressing the door." Inside were three inflatable life vests, one already fully inflated.

"You'll hear the whole of the safety talk when we gather for dinner. But rest assured, there have been no accidents at Valdes Underwater Resort."

Frankie really wanted to say something to that. But Evelyn Crowe wouldn't know anything different, so Frankie kept her mouth shut.

They strolled through one of the three big domes that made up the Research and Innovation Village. These had only small, porthole-style windows, and much of the space was closed into rooms and offices. But a garden was somewhere near: Frankie smelled sweet basil.

In the passageway from the village to the executive suites, Frankie caught her first glimpse of the chasm at the edge of the resort. Abyss, more like. Lights shone into it, but didn't get far.

Before stepping into the executive area, Valdes stopped.

"It's crucial that you adhere to the privacy guidelines," she began, her voice low and conspiratorial. "Do not ask others for their names. Avoid personal inquiries. Refrain from divulging information about yourself."

Frankie nodded. She'd read the voluminous forms her doppelgänger had apparently signed in her stead. "And what happens here, stays here?" she ventured, recalling the infamous tagline.

One corner of Valdes's lips quirked but her gaze on Frankie remained cool. "Precisely. What transpires during this weekend must remain strictly confidential. No exceptions." She waved Frankie and Spike to precede her into the VIP area.

From the tunnel, Frankie stepped into soft grass. The flooring —surely it was flooring—undulated softly. It lapped at her feet just the slightest bit.

A barely-there blend of moonflower and some wonderful alien spices teased her nose somehow both calming and invigorating. Soft music eddied in the room, melody and harmonies more felt than heard.

She breathed in air both crisp and clean, carrying a faint hint of ozone, as if the very essence of the sea has been infused into the atmosphere. This place was poetry.

Valdes cleared her throat. Frankie looked back. Spike sagged against the doorjamb, groan-sighing. Right. Frankie had to keep moving. She could stare at the amazing, so-soft floor later. Stare like a tourist, as rude Evelyn Crowe surely would.

"Lovely, isn't it?" Valdes said once they were all out of the hatchway and into the first open lounge area. Frankie had memorized the rough layout of the resort, but that lines-and-spaces view hadn't told her half the story.

When Frankie could finally drag her gaze from her feet and the floor, her attention was briefly caught by the striking balance of bleeding-edge technology and organic, naturalistic design elements. Swooping sofas and low tables, floating orbs radiating soft-white light near the seating and the inner walls.

But then her gaze was caught by the sweeping curve into the dining room, with its transparent aluminum walls offering a breathtaking view of the shallow shelf of coral leading to the vast stretch of deep darkness beyond the resort's edge.

"Our furnishings are a fusion of organic and sustainable synthetic materials," Vales said. "Bio-engineered woods and self-healing fabrics adjust to the contours of the body and react to your desires." She reached toward one of the lighted orbs; it floated to her. She swiped her hand across and back, and the orb grew dimmer or brighter. She set her palm over the orb, not touching it, and pushed her hand to hip level. The orb obediently followed, and there it remained.

Its now-brighter light bathed Spike in soft white. The cyvlossic, eyes closed, was swaying visibly now.

Frankie sighed. They would have all weekend here to explore, but Spike needed to get better now.

"We should go straight to our room," she said. "Precious is too much for me to lift, I'm afraid."

A movement among the deep seats arrayed near the wall on the other side of the dining-room entrance caught Frankie's eye. A masculine-presenting person in a perfectly tailored CapCity suit rose from one of the seats, an old-fashioned highball glass in one hand.

Valdes took Frankie by the elbow and started to steer her through the lounge, keeping maximum distance from the stranger. His presence had marred the first impression the resort was going for—a paradise for you alone.

The stranger was undaunted. His steps took him on a collision course with their small group.

"Well, well, well," he drawled, his voice a well-modulated tenor even under the resort's high pressure. The crinkled velvet blue of his suit—a day style tunic and narrow slacks—shimmered even under the soft lighting.

"Such a fresh face in our little underwater paradise." He pushed a strand of his long, platinum blond hair past his shoulder to fall with the rest smooth and straight nearly to his rear. So useless, in space and under water. So CapCity. "And so young!"

Frankie froze. He thought she was the victim?

Beside her, Valdes's chin dropped, a flicker of annoyance crossing her features. "Sir," she began, her tone a careful blend of politeness and warning. "I was explaining the protocols for the weekend to our new guests."

The man waved a dismissive hand, his sharp eyes never leaving Frankie's face. "I'm here so often everybody knows my name." He extended the hand towards Frankie, his movements fluid and graceful. "Nathan Henderson, at your service."

Frankie hesitated, glancing towards Valdes for guidance. The proprietor's face pretended cool detachment, but Frankie could see the tension in her jaw, the slight twitch of her fingers against her liquid metal dress.

"Mr. Henderson," Valdes said, her voice cooler than before. "I must insist that you respect the guidelines we have in place. They are for the comfort—and privacy—of all our guests. Especially this weekend, as you surely know."

Henderson rolled his eyes, a child's reaction at odds with his sophisticated appearance. "Come now, Monica," he chided. "Surely we can make an exception for such a lovely creature as this."

He didn't think Frankie would tell on him. Because she was the bait. Fury flushed up her neck.

Spike, sensing Frankie's rage even through her own pain, let out a low, warning growl. She bumped Frankie's knee.

Henderson's eyes flickered to Spike.

"My, my. Is that a cat or a pony?" He glanced at Valdes. "Does the judge know?" Valdes cleared her throat, perhaps masking a groan?

"Mr. Henderson," she said. "Every guest deserves their privacy. Every. Guest."

"Of course. Anything you want, Monica." Henderson tooke a slop sip of the green-gold liquid in his glass. Valdes, her hand still on Frankie's elbow, started moving toward the passageway ahead of them.

"Until next time, my dear," Henderson said behind them, his voice a silken caress recognizable to any femme in CapCity. "I look forward to getting to know you better."

As they stepped into the passageway, Valdes did something with her hand that made the air buzz. A privacy screen?

"I apologize for Mr. Henderson's behavior," she said, her voice so lovely it made the words a song. "He is a treasured guest."

Frankie, confused, merely nodded. A killer-weekend guest who made repeat visits? Ick.

She needed to find out more about him.

Chapter Nine

Entering the passage that led to each guest's private dome, Frankie, wound tight by Nathan Henderson's faux familiarity, was sharp enough to notice the subtle shift in the resort's color palette. These walls took on a deep, rich hue of midnight blue, accented by thin veins of shimmering, iridescent material that resembled the bioluminescent patterns the brochure described were in the abyssal depths. Super-fancy nightlights, these.

"Evelyn" had apparently requested that she be given the dome farthest from the entrance, even though the better rooms were closer. It was a bit of a walk, but had the advantage of being directly beside one of the emergency escape submersibles.

Monica Valdes led them to the last deceptively simple-looking sliding door, number sixteen.

"Here we are," she announced, her voice a sultry whisper. As the golden metallic door slid down, she stepped to the side.

Frankie stepped inside, her eyes widening as she took in the opulent surroundings. The place was three-quarters windows, showing the open sea, a bit of sand-garden to one side and the abyss to the other.

Beside her, narrow charcoal-swirled walls and a pocket door hid a bathroom, on one side of the main door. On the other side, a walk-in closet already held her travel duffels. Frankie drifted right past these, drawn by the breathtaking view. The flooring matched that of the lounge area, mossy and swirling, only in darker tones. Frankie's feet demanded to be set free from her stylish gravboots right now.

Spike stumbled onto the bed, which swayed slightly. As the hefty lump of cyvlossic dropped onto the mattress, it conformed to her shape. The tufted cottony tan blanket on top tucked into Spike like a warm hug.

Monica Valdes leaned against the far corner of the closet. "Some rest will do wonders for your companion's adjustment to the environment."

The bed frame matched the golden metal of the doors. It seemed to float above the floor. Frankie bent down to look under the bed.

"Antigravity pads," Valdes said. "If you choose, the beds will gently sway with the rhythm of the sea. But it might be better to wait until you're all feeling better."

She gestured to the wall hiding the closet. "The screen gives you control of all of the room's features. Lights, bed, sound, temperature, even smell. And here," she swiped up to show a pictographic menu. "You can turn the walls opaque or transparent, or anywhere in between."

Frankie spun in the center of the room. This assignment sucked but wow, she was glad she got to see this.

Valdes smiled at her enthusiasm. "You have the run of the resort. As you know, you are one of only sixteen guests here this weekend. We're doing maintenance on the more-general areas, but I know you like to jog, so feel free to include those on your route."

Oh yeah, she supposedly liked to jog. Frankie nodded in a way she hoped looked enthusiastic. It was a smart hobby, for someone who wanted to check out every cranny of this place. Because someone was about to die here, she reminded herself.

Valdes was wrapping up. "We do ask that you stay in this area just until dinner. That's when we do the formal safety review." Her honeyed voice grew a bit more rote. "I trust you will find everything to your—"

A sound at the dome's entrance started them. Valdes turned as fast as an eel.

A gray-haired femme-presenting person stood panting in the entryway. She could have been Frankie's cousin—short, thick, and solid, wearing baggy gray sweatpants and a dark, wet-splattered t-shirt.

"Doctor?" Vales said. This must be the marine biologist, Natasha Mazur. SystA had given Frankie a list of most-likely people who would be on staff this weekend. Over two-thirds of the more than three hundred staffers had the past week and weekend off, supposedly taking a break from the pressure.

"Problem—issue, I mean—with the carcharodon pod," Mazur wheezed. Her vocal cords had not been modified for underwater pressure.

At the word "problem," Valdes stiffened. Obviously there were never problems at her resort. She stepped toward Mazur, appearing to push her out of Frankie's room merely with the force of her aura.

"If you'll excuse me," Valdes said, glancing back at Frankie. "Enjoy your rest. We'll meet again at dinner, at six."

Valdes glided out of the room and into the corridor, continuing to herd Mazur in front of her. The door slid up, closing Frankie and Spike in their bubble of a room.

Frankie stood motionless for a moment, and then dropped into one of the three reclining sand-like seats that faced the windows. The slightly nubbly fabric on the bench molded itself to her shape. It eased the slight twinge in the small of her back, but did not ease the weight of their mission upon her shoulders.

Nathan Henderson, creep, expected to watch someone die. Monica Valdes, semi-aquatic cypher, must have something to do with it.

Spike stirred on the bed, her eyes fluttering open.

"Intense," she rasped.

"You said it." Frankie kicked Evelyn's fancy high-heeled grav-boots off. She stretched out her legs, flexing her feet. The bottom section of the recliner lifted to meet them.

Wow, she could get used to this.

Frankie called up a screen and sent a quick, coded message to the blind address that SystA had set up for this assignment, telling Bruce, or Gem, or whoever picked it up that they were in.

Over the next hour, she reviewed all SystA knew about who was here on the resort. She'd start matching faces to names at the pre-dinner safety lecture. Everyone—all the guests, at least—were required to attend the briefing.

But soon enough, Frankie was deep into the dining-room menu, the diving schedule, the list of lectures. "Comparative coral groups" had a lecture and then a dive!

But she couldn't get too comfortable. She was here to do a job, the one that she'd failed at up on Shepherd Station.

Then again, maybe she could. If she could get a tag on Aimee Samson right away, SystA's divers maybe could sweep in overnight and spirit the girl to safety. The guilty parties would expose them-selves, trying to quickly solve the lost-girl problem before the paying clients noticed. After that, Frankie would have almost a day just to frolic.

One could always hope.

Finally, Spike started to snore. Frankie's shoulders eased. She must have been waiting for that sound. Frankie tried to think of Spike's snoring as a low hum, but it was really more like a small chainsaw. Up top; now, underwater, it was more like a train whistle.

But it meant Spike was feeling better. Frankie could do this job herself, but Spike's presence as backup was a comfort. Comfort animal, indeed.

Her wristcom chimed. Quarter of an hour till showtime.

She pushed off the decadent recliner and headed toward the closet. Time to try out another of Evelyn's outfits. Maybe the slacks, with the lower-heeled boots.

Time to meet more suspects.

Chapter Ten

Under the cool glow of bioluminescent lights, fourteen of the sixteen Elysium Weekend guests gathered in the VIP lounge near the entry to the underwater resort's executive dining room.

The orbs' shifting colors cast an ethereal aura over the oddly quiet group, which looked to be mostly couples. Each unit, single or pair, stood separate from the others, as if everyone was afraid of catching some virus. Actually, they probably didn't want to see what kind of people would pay to watch someone die.

And to recognize themselves in those others.

Frankie, stiff in her formal floor-length sheath dress, pretended not to stare at everyone while staring at everyone. And she wiggled her bare toes in the grassy carpeting. Her new, exorbitantly priced sandals, purchased from the resort's catalog, were easy to slide out of. Surreptitiously slide out of, Frankie hoped. The resort probably had a shoes-on dining room policy. Then again, Monica Valdes hadn't been wearing shoes.

Spike, sitting beside Frankie like a normal companion animal, shifted to the front, and sat on her feet. Before Frankie could react, a tall, lean person strode into their midst from the Tech Village side of the dome.

Sylvana Patel, head of safety, could turn heads. Beautiful deep brown skin, dark eyes to drown in, and the glossiest of loose curls fighting to free themselves from an elastic scrunchie at her nape.

Like Monica Valdes, Patel had a fluid understanding of the term uniform. Her sleeveless, hip-hugging one-piece white pantsuit, its legs flaring, did not scream security. The chunky gray utility belt, though, a playful interpretation of the belts divers wore, gave the game away. Most of its square box-pockets were snapped closed, but that black extendable baton looked fearsome.

Patel did not hide the jagged double scar on her right forearm. She used the arm to wave for attention, as if she did not have it already. The guests formed an awkward half-circle around her, all at least a meter away from that scar.

"Esteemed guests, welcome," she said without a smile. "I am Sylvana Patel, head of security and safety. Just as you do on a marine vessel or a spacecraft, we will have a short discussion of the safety measures and procedures here at Valdes Resort."

"As you see, we are situated within a series of domes and passageways nearly two hundred meters below the sea. While our facilities are designed with your safety in mind, it's crucial that you follow some basic guidelines."

Frankie accepted a fluted glass of something bubbly from a server dressed in burgundy velvet.

"Just sparkling ula berry," they said to her unspoken question. "We want you to remember the lecture."

Frankie missed the next part of the lecture anyway. Monica Valdes glided to her side, striking in a simple silver wrap dress that made the blue in her skin glow. She knelt to stroke Spike. Spike would normally have slashed her hand red. Spike as Precious, thankfully, held back.

Frankie dropped to Spike's other side protectively.

"So well behaved," Valdes said softly. She pulled her hand away, resting it on her knee. "I apologize for asking this of you, but one of our guests has a rather severe allergy to cats." Valdex unconsciously glanced over to a tiny gray-haired angry-looking person in a two-piece gray CapCity femme suit. "Is it possible for you to do without Precious, just at mealtimes?"

Frankie pretended to be thinking. Let Spike loose, to roam the whole of the resort, while everyone else was together in one room? Couldn't be a better setup for investigating this place. She looked at "Precious."

Spike head-butted Frankie's knee. Frankie telegraphed that she was coming in for a hug, and wrapped her arms around Spike's soft shoulders. Already, she could feel a bit of matting along the shoulders.

"I suppose," Frankie sighed. She rolled back up to standing and waved toward the guest room passageway. "Precious, go home." This would only work if Valdes knew so little about companion animals that she wouldn't recognize that there was no "home" here.

It worked. With a casual flick of her tail, "Precious" sauntered out of the room, her gray-on-black fur blending into the shadows as she crossed into the passageway. Spike didn't have to be asked twice. She'd take full advantage of her newfound freedom, exploring every nook and cranny of this place.

Valdes rose gracefully. She touched Frankie's elbow lightly.

"You're safe with us," she said, her eyes warm and so, so honest.

What a performance.

Security chief Patel's voice had paused. She was touching her wristcom. A hologram of the resort appeared between her and the guests. She continued.

"In addition to the rebreathers and warm-wraps tucked next to every door, please take note of the locations of the exit submersibles. There are four nearest us." She pointed on the model. "Here at the side of Tech Village, there are two. Here, at the end of your guest room hall, one." She pointed to the one next door to Frankie's room. "Also at the end of every corridor. No corridors have dead ends."

A couple people chuckled, not sure if Patel had made a joke.

She had not. "Each submersible can hold up to twenty people," she said sternly. "Very cramped. We have never, in fifteen years, had to use one. Thanks to you, your knowledge and good preparation, this is why we don't have such incidents. We are grateful for your attention."

The security chief certainly had the patter down pat for someone whom the resort had hired on only two months ago. SystA was still searching for information on the last head of resort security, but not with that much effort. If the killings were still going on at the resort, it wasn't likely that the former chief had done it.

But they could have had a part in it.

Frankie's eyes wandered back to the small, severe gray-haired woman. Who could such a person be, that she would come here, alone, to see something that promised to be so gruesome?

While most of the guests pretended to pay attention, it was clear they were more interested in the delicious smells emanating from the dining room's kitchen or trying to wave down the server for a "real" drink. But gray woman hung on every word, her sharp gaze focused intently on the head of security as she described the submersibles.

Nathan Henderson's strong cologne—bergamot and alcohol—

preceded him. Late to the party, he sauntered directly into Frankie's space, stopping only a couple centimeters from her shoulder. Frankie moved her face, but her gaze didn't move as fast. Henderson saw the object of her attention.

"Ah, the judge," Henderson whispered conspiratorially. "Second time for our girl."

That woman was a judge? An officer of the law? On what planet?

Valdes appeared at Henderson's other side, her face barely masking disapproval.

"Gotta run," Henderson said. "My sweetie's getting mad." He allowed Valdes to pull him aside. They both sat on the closest of those sandy benches, which formed itself to their twosome. Very cozy.

Beyond the bench, Frankie spotted a solitary figure hovering near the edge of the gathering.

Aimee Sansom. At last.

Sansom stood out among the guests, her discomfort plain even from a distance. She had colored her blond hair auburn, and cut most of it off. Now the so-straight strands reached only just under her chin. Contacts made her eyes a dull brown. Her wrap dress was the same style as Valdes had on, burnt bronze to the resort proprietor's bright silver. But on Sansom the dress hung wrong. Not enough meat.

Henderson caught sight of her, and sat up straight. His gaze locked on the girl.

The victim.

Before he could stand, Frankie had moved to intercept. Protective.

She gave the girl her untasted flute glass.

"Sparkling ula berry?" she said. "It gives me the hiccups."

Sansom almost smiled. She took the glass in her beautifully

manicured fingers. She wore the kind of makeup that young women wore who wanted to pretend they weren't wearing makeup.

"I think I missed the lecture," she said.

Of course she had. She must have heard it yesterday, when she arrived.

"No worries," Frankie said. "Mostly it was just run to the doorways, where all the emergency supplies are hidden. And if that doesn't work, run for one of the submersibles."

"Those round things? There's one two doors down from me."

So Sansom was in room fourteen. Good to know. Frankie fumbled for the pocket in her dress for the tin of tiny tracker tags. No time like the present to tag her target.

The dress was too tight. Frankie couldn't slide her hand in without looking like she had fleas or something.

Plan B.

"Pardon me," she said, putting on her best Evelyn Crow demeanor. "I couldn't help but notice you're here on your own, too. Would you like some company for dinner?" That would give her plenty of time to arrange a light touch.

Sansom's eyes widened in surprise. For a moment, her expression eased, and it looked like she would accept Frankie's offer.

But just as quickly, her face shifted back to anxiety and fear.

Before Frankie could react, Sansom mumbled an excuse and backed away. Frankie, puzzled, watched her hurry toward Monica Valdes, who was now standing beside the gray lady.

Then Frankie noticed the hulking man at her elbow.

The drinks server from before.

"Follow me," he said. "Your table is ready."

More than an hour later, Frankie was surprised at how full a person could get on seaweed salads, fancy fish broth and seared shark. She set aside a portion of the shark for Spike; she didn't think the salad would be as much of a hit.

She lingered over the ula berry gelée, gazing out across the abyss. The darting fish had apparently gone home for the night. She couldn't see how they could tell; the water at this level always looked dark to her.

Most of the other guests had departed—Aimee Sansom first of all, ugh. But an easygoing man in a loose white shirt and tight pants had been traveling from table to table, speaking briefly to each guest, and she could see she was next. And, after one so-sharp glass of wine, she was curious.

"Ma'am, may I?" the man said, smiling so wide, and took a seat. "Samir Russo. Pleased to meet you."

The diving instructor. Of course.

"I understand you've brought your own equipment," he said, looking at an actual piece of paper. He looked up at her. "Experienced diver?"

She shook her head. "A gift, from an experienced diver."

"Right," Russo said. His pretty brown hair was cut too short for the curls to catch a break. "I'll check it over with you tomorrow, before we go, no problem."

Frankie couldn't help smiling back. Then she remembered: he could be the actual killer.

She struggled to keep the friendly in her face.

"I'm interested in everything!" she said, a little loud. "The coral looks so cool. And outside my room there's this—it looks like a maze."

"The labyrinth," he said. "Isn't it a beautiful spot?" He leaned back in the chair, completely at ease. His shoulders were so wide he could probably swim the ocean in one go. "We'll get you there."

Frankie had to shake her head to keep up.

No more drinking. She sat straight in her chair and reached for the napkin-covered teacup containing Spike's dinner. Time to go.

"One more thing, just," Russo said. "You're a single, and everyone diving must have a partner. I could dive with you, or Dr. Mazur could. But it would be better for you to partner with the other single who is diving. Would that be okay with you?"

"Who is it?" Not Henderson.

"I don't know her name," he said, lying graciously. "She's the young one who was wearing one of Monica's dresses."

Aimee Sansom.

"I know her," Frankie said. "She seemed very ... alert. That will be fine."

"Perfect!" Russo rose as Frankie did. "Dive prep starts at ten, but there's going to be a great talk by Dr. Mazur about coral, and fish—and maybe a surprise, too. We can learn, and then go!"

"Yes." Frankie tested her balance. Thank Safra she was wearing these flat sandals, even if they had given her a a little blister on one heel. "That does sounds perfect."

The long walk to her guest room helped clear her head. And the thought, as she felt the constant pulse and pull of the ocean above her and around her, that down here, she was prey.

Stepping over the down-sliding entry door, Frankie was already trying to unfasten this absolute sheath of a dress as she stepped into the walk-in closet. She waved the light brighter.

And almost stepped on a single diving glove. Caked with what looked like blood.

Chapter Eleven

The airlock leading to the diving preparation room took itself very seriously. Yellow lights, red symbols, voice warnings, extra pushes of the open button before it actually clicked open, the whole deal.

When Frankie finally stepped through the opening, feeling as if she'd solved some tricky puzzle, all she got for her effort was the bite of a lungful of brine.

Oh, yeah, they were deep underwater. She'd been looking out at it for half a day now, but the resort was so posh her brain must have decided the walls were fancy vid screens, her squeaky voice an odd affect, Spike's headache just a headache. Nothing to worry about.

Here, tasting the salt in the air, seeing the big open pool at the far edge of the dome, reality hit back. The airlock did a great job holding the humidity at bay. It kept the rest of the resort from feeling steamy or musty. That, and probably some giant dehumidifiers.

Behind her, the door slammed shut. She was the last of the

morning crowd to enter. Only Frankie and the judge had come early to listen to Dr. Mazur's talk about the daytime flora and fauna. Both Frankie and the judge wore tank swimsuits under a so-fluffy bathrobe provided by the resort. Frankie's robe somehow matched her suit, a dusty rose. She'd wondered if the judge's suit was as gray as her robe.

But mostly she'd wondered where the heck Spike was. After dropping that bloody clue in her lap (okay, on the floor), Spike had been less than forthcoming.

She said she'd found it here, in the diving room, but who knew where? No, she wouldn't show Frankie until morning, when more people were around to see. Their job was to tag Aimee Sansom, and only secondarily to gather clues. They couldn't rush ahead with the clues and chance that they would miss Sansom a second time.

Frankie hadn't said anything after that. Especially not that she'd already missed Sansom a second time, at dinner.

But the anticipation had not been good for her sleep. And then, when Frankie had finally given up on sleep and rose in the half-light of an underwater dawn, Spike had been gone.

Some companion animal.

Above the diving room's dome the ocean was a dusky blue-green. Full day topside, this was as bright as it got down here. A large school of thin fish—bait—drifted by, casting rippling shadows.

Close to the entry was an open space, enough to collect two dozen or so eager divers and herd them to the double corral of wide wood-veneer lockers on either side. Two couples, Nathan Henderson, the judge, Frankie, and Aimee Sansom were the only eager divers this morning.

No one had moved more than a meter into the room. Perhaps they'd all had the same feeling: Small and soft, about to face the mighty pressures of the deep.

"Good morning, everyone!" Samir Russo called out, his voice booming through the room. He stepped out from around the edge of one of the double banks of lockers, already suited up except for air tanks and helmet. Aimee Sansom, standing next to Henderson at the front, took a half-step back.

Frankie stopped herself from doing the same. Could this friendly-looking bear of a man be the Killer of Valdes Underwater Resort? He had the opportunity.

She shivered, and pulled her fuzzy bathrobe tighter. She slid her toes past the edge of the resort-provided flip-flops and curled them into the short pile of the mossy carpet under her feet.

"Welcome to our little pool." Russo waved toward the length of water at the far end of the dome, and waited for the chuckle that did not come. "This is where the magic happens, where we embark on our thrilling journey into the twilight depths of our sea."

Still no reaction.

"Right. So, everybody drops from here, so we can keep track of you going and coming. That's our friend Sylvana's job. You met her last night. She's already back there, see? Getting ready for us.

"Once outside, first thing we do is point out all the many, many markers that will guide you right back home. No worries, all awesomeness, that's our motto."

A truly impressive array of equipment hung on racks beyond the lockers and lining the walls. Wetsuits made from advanced nano- and polymaterials hung on shiny metal racks. Some of the suits incorporated something like fish scales that glinted under the artificial light.

Thick dive masks crowded with tech sat on shelves next to the racks, their lenses promising unparalleled clarity and integrated heads-up displays. Other, simpler masks promised a view with fewer complications. The air tanks must be on the far side.

"We've matched your locker numbers to your room numbers,"

Russo said. "See? I chose the equipment I think will suit you best. But as you can see, we have lots of options if you find anything uncomfortable or too troublesome." He waved toward the racks. "Now let's get you suited up and ready to go!"

Frankie's room number blinked on the wide wood-veneer door of a locker in the right locker cul-de-sac. Aimee Sansom's locker was two down from Frankie's. Everyone had plenty of space.

Russo, moved among the guests in the left set of lockers. Smile wide, ably assisting them in managing all their gear. Nothing about him triggered any warnings, which set Frankie on edge. Could a person be too friendly? Of course, but this wasn't like the CapCity political crowd.

Frankie unwillingly slipped off the plush bathrobe. Without that—and without Spike—she felt exposed. But the equipment in the locker was familiar. Everything Bruce and SystA had sent was here.

She stepped into the suit with no problems, but the inner hood was another matter.

"Here, let me help you with that," Russo offered, his voice friendly and, thankfully, softer, as he approached. His suit smelled the slightest bit musty. "Just hold your hair back for me, and voilà."

His gaze traveled up the sleek, black material of her two-layer suit, lingering on the knobby carbon-fiber buttons that closed the neck. His smile was teasing.

"See you've gone for a spacer's style. Quite the state-of-the-art choice, with that shiny coating, but not what us sea divers usually go for." He picked up her helmet and pointed out the differences, mostly the shape of the visor—big and square instead of oval or round—and how the controls worked. Spacers needed big buttons; divers usually didn't.

His fingers skimmed over the material as he spoke. Frankie

remained still, working to stay calm. What had this man's hands done to other women?

"Of course, it'll still a great dive suit," Russo said reassuringly. "Wouldn't want to really wear it in space, heh. It'll work perfectly for our excursion today."

When he reached for Frankie's face, she couldn't stop her flinch.

He had something in his hand.

"Sorry," she stammered, trying to cover her reaction. "It's just... the suit feels strange."

"No worries," he said. "This will help. It's a skin-bound communications device. There are four channels. I'll always be on Channel One." He reached for her face again. Now Frankie recognized the shape, a curved bit of sticky tape with wiring tucked inside. Russo spread it along her jaw on the left side.

"You've used one of these before?" Russo asked. Frankie nodded. "Same as all the others then. Open channel with your tongue, one tap. Close, two taps."

Frankie's gaze flicked over to Sansom, who seemed to be testing different ways of twisting her hair up before slipping the suit's hood on. She already had the sticky microphone setup along her jaw.

If Russo could stick something on the woman, then Frankie could, too. Now was the time to get that stupid tag on her.

Russo turned to the gray lady. Her suit seemed to have bits missing.

Now was Frankie's chance. The tin of tiny tracking devices was easy to reach, in a pocket of her robe. She stuck one to a fingertip and turned it on. Then she turned to Sansom.

"Let me help you with that," she said to the woman, still fussing with her hair. "Best just to push it all back, from the forehead, and hold it. Yes, like that."

Frankie started pulling the tight head covering up Sansom's neck, and then over the woman's hands as she held her hair at the nape. A little jiggle as Sansom pulled her hands out gave Frankie the opening she needed.

One of the fine strands had come out with the hands. Frankie lifted it between two of her fingers and tucked it back in, depositing the tracking chip behind Sansom's ear in the process.

"Your hair is so fine," Frankie said, hoping to distract the woman. "Baby soft."

"Bad nutrition," the woman said. "No, seriously. Thank you. I'm a little nervous. Have you dived before?"

"Only in vacuum, never in liquid." Frankie finished pulling the hood over, trying not to snap it on Sansom's forehead. "You?"

"Just a little snorkeling." She shivered. Too thin. Too pale.

"This suit is supposed to have a warmer," she said. "But Samir said not to use it until we feel the water outside. He says the water is warmer than you'd think."

Frankie wasn't cold, but she knew the feeling. Anxiety. Fear. She looked at Sansom's locker. Her fluffy robe was bright red.

"Why don't we wear our robes, over? Stay warm until the last minute."

"Think we can?"

"What can they say? No?" Frankie shrugged. "No worries, all awesomeness."

That choked a laugh out of the woman.

When everyone was decked out, they collected again closer to the pool. Russo and Sylvana Patel stood between a solid metal table and a series of similar shelves, most with paired air tanks on them. Patel's wetsuit didn't cover half her legs or arms. The shark bite along her forearm looked even harsher than last night.

Patel had been bitten while saving a fellow diver back when she was in the military, or so Dr. Mazur had told them this morning.

Mazur said if you could get close enough, you could even tell the mature teeth marks from the baby teeth marks.

Frankie didn't see the need to get so close to the resort's security chief, a very likely co-conspirator in the killings. Not to mention, Patel was still wearing that scary baton from last night.

And where in Safra's great universe was Spike?

Patel pulled an air tank down from the shelves, set it on the waist-high table with a clank, and checked its gauges and hoses. Satisfied, she slid the equipment down to Russo and went to get another.

"Step up!" Russo said. "The tanks are all the same. It's your masks that are different, but the connection's the same."

Aimee Sansom stepped up first. She lay her robe on the edge of the table away from the action and then placed herself in front of Russo.

"We have a winner!" Russo teased, signaling her to turn around. He did up the tank straps in less than thirty seconds, even with the double-checking. Sansom placed her narrow oval of a mask over her face, and Russo tightened its straps in the back. He leaned closer to her ear, now covered in diving suit and mask straps.

"Air okay?"

She nodded and then remembered to give him the sign: thumb's up. He handed her a pair of flippers and pointed toward the pool. She wobbled to the pool, dark and still. Around the inside was a narrow shelf about half a meter down, perfect for setting flippered feet on. But Sansom sat at the pool's edge facing away from the water. She obviously wasn't going to be the first in everything.

Frankie hung back, keeping an eye out for Spike. Soon enough, everyone would be gone or distracted. It wouldn't be safe enough for just the two of them to out a suspect.

She felt a tap on her shoulder and turned around to face a lean woman with cybernetic augmentations that outlined her dark eyes like metallic makeup. Her short, black hair glittered under the artificial lighting. The woman lifted a hand in sort of a mini-wave.

"Jin Watike. I couldn't help but notice your suit. Quite the prize."

"Thanks?" Frankie said. "Samir told me it was a bit different."

Watike's angular face was not beautiful, but striking. Memorable, even without the eye accents. Her eyes, mesmerizing, seemed to drink in every detail. Her marine blue dive suit shimmered with those intricate fish-scale style metallic patterns. In addition to the below-the-jaw comms device, Watike wore a wrist display and had various tools strapped to her belt.

"Different is an understatement." Watike examined the material and accessories closely. "The graphene weave combined with flexi-armor is quite unusual. Very strong. Interesting."

Frankie suddenly remembered her cover identity. Clueless heiress.

"Oh yes, my personal stylist had it custom made."

"But by whom? Surely you know. No label."

Frankie shrugged, clueless heiresslike. For a moment, Watike frowned, like a crack of thunder, but quickly wiped it away. Frankie played dumb.

"I don't remember seeing you last night," she said. "At the safety lecture." With that hair, the woman would have been hard to miss.

"I was working," Watike said casually, as if working two hundred meters underwater was nothing out of the ordinary. "Besides, I designed most of the safety features throughout the resort. It's my business."

Now Frankie frowned. SystA had thought that all the tech village would be emptied this weekend. Obviously not.

"How many people work with you?" she said.

"None, this weekend." Watike grimaced. "Which gives me time for diving. They're all gallivanting on the beaches up-top. Giving their blood and bodies a rest from all this pressure."

"You don't gallivant?"

Watike laughed. Frankie couldn't tell if her voice had been altered to counteract the pressure. It was a high soprano, but clear.

"Not this weekend. Say—" At the sound of someone shuffling up, Watike looked around, and frowned. Nathan Henderson, diving suit as slick as the rest of him.

"Jin! I came up with a new slogan for your firm," Henderson said.

"No."

"No, really, listen. 'Want it unique? Then chose Watike.' It even rhymes."

"Are you kidding?"

"Okay, how about make it shorter: 'Watike means unique.' Or equals—you could use the symbol. That screams 'tech giant,' right?"

"Say," Watike said, looking at Frankie. "You wouldn't want to switch partners, would you? Henderson's an ass, but he's a good diver. Knows the best spots."

Absolutely not.

"Sorry," Frankie said, faking an apologetic tone. "My partner is already nervous. I don't want to change anything at the last minute."

Watike sighed.

"I tried," she said. Her gaze finally left Frankie's suit and took in her face. "Younger than you look, aren't you?"

Ice trickled down Frankie's spine. This woman thought she was this weekend's victim.

Even in her robe, Frankie's whole body went cold. She had to get away from Jin Watike.

Frankie turned back, turning at the last moment to not look at Sansom and instead look at Russo. He was free, for a moment, while one of the couples decide which one should go first.

"I'm up," she said. "See you in the water." She scooted past the couple, dropped her robe on the table beside Sansom's and got into position in front of Russo.

She never wanted someone to look at her like that again. Hungry.

Eager.

The weight of the tanks on her back was actually a comfort. As Russo worked the straps tight, he leaned forward to whisper.

"Thanks again for pairing up today. I've been working on one of our regulars, trying to get her in the water. She's finally taking me up on the offer, so we'll be co-diving today."

Why did that make Frankie feel even less safe? She murmured her thanks.

"Hey, Henderson, need a hand?" Jin Watike said. "Time's a wasting."

"Yeah, I know," he said, finally stepping up to the now-shorter line. "And no."

"Suit yourself," Jin quipped, rolling her eyes.

Frankie still had her mask in her hands when she saw the gray-and-black blur.

Spike. Finally.

The cyvlossic was rocketing along the wall, avoiding the lights, avoiding the divers.

Frankie turned to follow Spike's progress.

"Whoa," Russo said, looking at Frankie's face. "Too tight?" He reached for the strap across Frankie's collarbone.

Spike reached the tall set of shelves, now with a few empty spots where air tanks had been, and leapt to the highest shelf. She really was like a cat sometimes.

"Trouble with the mask?" Russo hadn't seen anything. Neither had Patel, busy reading gauges on the next set of air tanks.

Frankie opened her mouth and took a breath. What could she say?

Near where Spike had been, a large gray, rubber-looking bin crashed to the floor.

Everybody jumped.

The bin had hit on its side, dislodging its sturdy-looking lid. Old, broken diving gear tumbled out, alongside fragments of what looked like bloodstained fabric.

A slow-moving gasp traveled the room as each person turned to look and then recognized what they were seeing.

Frankie swore she could smell the blood. So many pieces of it. So many objects.

Something from every girl?

And he'd kept them, like souvenirs. She'd heard that about serial killers, the collecting they did.

"People get mauled here?" Frankie choked out, her voice trembling. "Murdered?"

All eyes turned to Samir Russo, expressions a mixture of accusation and disbelief.

The cautiously excited atmosphere had evaporated, leaving a chilling tension in its wake.

"Please, everyone!" Russo implored, his deep voice cracking under the weight of the room's scrutiny. "It's not what it looks like!"

Chapter Twelve

"It's not what it looks like!"

Samir Russo's desperate plea echoed through the stunned silence of the diving prep room. Frankie couldn't stop staring at the sheer amount of bloodstained diving gear that had fallen out of the bin.

The fresh-salt tang in the air had evaporated, replaced by dank taste of tension. Frankie pulled her gaze off the evidence and looked around the room.

The other divers, frozen in various states of readiness, stared at Russo with a mixture of uncertainty and accusation in their eyes.

Sylvana Patel, finishing up her examination of a set of air tanks, seemed to be the only one unfazed by the grim discovery.

But she wasn't saying anything.

"This is... this is old gear, from long ago," Russo said. "It's not—"

Frankie could see his words weren't working. Russo stopped, and started again. He stepped around Frankie, away from the bin, closer to the guests seated around the edge of the diving pool.

"As you know, underwater diving can be dangerous," he said pleadingly. "We do everything we can to ensure our guests' safety, but sometimes, we can tell, people don't listen."

"So we made these up." He waved at Patel, who stooped down to pick up a fin. She held it up. It looked like a small shark had bitten a semicircle out of it.

A perfect semicircle.

"It's blood, yes," Russo said. "But from our kitchens. And the rips and tears, that's just plain old hard use. Nobody wearing any of this equipment was ever harmed."

Patel held her arm out, the arm a real shark had taken a bite out of. It was not a perfect semicircle. She held the torn fin close to her scar. Nothing like.

Patel tipped the bin back up with her foot, and dropped the flipper into it.

"But," Sansom started.

"Why?" Frankie finished.

"This is our 'scare the kids' box," Russo said. "You know, teenagers and other folks who we can tell aren't taking things seriously enough. We pull out a couple of these baddies, talk about the danger, maybe imply something awful has happened in the past. And let their imaginations run with it." He shrugged, sheepish. "That's it."

Russo looked around at the divers, nearly all far above twenty years old. "Remember being a kid? You think you're invincible."

"A kid? I still felt that way in my thirties."

A few people smiled slightly. A couple chuckled to each other. They must have kids.

"Right," Patel finally chimed in. "We get families here, on the regular weekends. Always one clown in the bunch. We just want everyone to take safety seriously."

That made more sense than the idea that there was a serial killer holding onto keepsakes by storing them in some old rubber bin in a public diving room.

Frankie caught a movement on the top of the shelves. Spike, in the shadows.

She nodded to her colleague, and then shrugged her shoulders. Spike also nodded. Russo was off the top of the suspect list.

For now.

Russo noticed something in the distance, and visibly relaxed.

"Ah, here's Dr. Mazur, with the surprise I promised last night." He stepped back to the table, ready to load air tanks onto the last two divers, Nathan Henderson and Jin Watike.

Frankie donned her mask, checked that air was flowing, gave Patel a thumb's up, and carried her flippers and diving gloves with her to the edge of the pool. She sat down facing the pool, and put her feet in the water. Sure there was a shelf for people's feet, but she could barely reach it with her toes. This world was built for tall people, too.

Sansom touched her tongue to her cheek, opening the audio channel.

"There's a shorter shelf over on that side," she said.

Everyone but the four at the air tanks heard her, and looked toward Frankie.

Great.

Frankie stayed where she was. No way she was going over to the kids' side. That shelf was even painted with baby fish or something.

Dr. Mazur, fully suited up except for her flippers, had both the flippers and one of the big rubbery bins, lid on, in her hands. She might be small and gray, but she was strong. Whatever was in the bin was moving, trying to knock her off balance.

She stomped over to the kiddie side of the pool and sat down. She set the bin on the shelf, covering up a couple little painted fishes. She lifted the lid.

Everyone leaned over to look.

It was a miniature monster shark. No a monstrush shark, specially adapted to the waters of the planet Kitt, where the temperatures varied widely from season to season.

Only about a meter long and squirmy like the eels Frankie had watched dance outside her window last night, this shark would grow to a fearsome eight or ten meters—the size of a personal submarine if it lived long enough.

So she did remember something from Mazur's lecture this morning.

"This little baby got herself caught up in out water-intake nets," Mazur said. "We're going to see if we can lure her mama out to come pick her up."

The marine biologist dropped her fins onto the shelf and slid her feet into them. She pulled out a thin cord and deftly tied a sliding knot along it.

"Each shark has a unique signature whistle, for individual identification," she said, going into lecture mode. "We're not sure how old they need to be to get their whistle, but I'm pretty sure mama will know any call they make."

She slipped the noose over the perfect gray-blue snout of the shark, slid it down until it rested between a weird bump and the upright fin in the shark's middle back.

"Who's with me? We'll go straight to the fence, and then double back to the squid farm."

Frankie looked a question at Sansom, who nodded. Who could pass this up?

Apparently everyone else except Nathan Henderson and Jin Watike.

Mazur set the lid back on the baby shark's bin. She'd cut holes in both the bin and the lid for waterflow.

Russo came around to her and double-checked her mask and

air. He was wearing that three-air-tank getup that the diver in the snuff video had worn. A piggy-back tank. The gray judge must be swimming free, like the victims she had watched did.

Frankie shuddered.

Not her circus. Just her assignment.

Security chief Patel came up to Sansom, checking her air systems. Satisfied, she checked Frankie's, Henderson's, and Watike's.

Mazur had slid in and was treading water, one hand on the shelf, one on the bin. Her small school of divers followed suit.

The water was warmer than she expected.

And thicker.

Until her face dropped below the water line, Frankie hadn't thought much about the dive itself. She'd been focused on tagging her target, fretting about Spike, plotting how to handle things if they had actually found the killer.

Now, she had none of those things to think about.

She only had the water.

And everything in it.

Just as Frankie touched the sand below the pool, one of those tube-fish banged her elbow. They were kind of grotty in the daytime, without their luminescence. And more solid than she'd thought. At least it wasn't a school of them, clumsy lumberers.

Mazur waited for them outside the dome. She pointed out the very obvious red and green arrows on all the posts and pylons supporting the domes, as well as all the standalone sticks with arrows, each pointing to the diving dome. She made eye contact with each diver, confirming that they were okay, and then repeated the process over the subvocal communications system.

They followed her along the side of the resort, past the tech village. She veered up a bit to show them the outside view of their own dining room. Two velvet-coated servers were setting the tables for dinner, and waved at them.

Frankie stuck with Sansom, which had her huffing and puffing in no time. The woman had great flipper skills. Henderson and Watike, behind them, must have switched to one of the other comm channels. They seemed to be arguing about something, with much hand waving, which was slowing them down.

The only sign that they'd reached the barrier was the vertical poles stretching far overhead. Even right up to the force field Frankie couldn't see it. No displacement of the water, nothing.

Of course, the cliff of the abyss, only a meter beyond the poles, also was a sign that they were at the end of the safe zone. The water beyond looked thirty percent darker.

Mazur set the bin on the sand and waited for the two slowboats to arrive.

"Our protective fence is one-way, for large creatures," she said over the main comms channel. "Once our little friend crosses, she won't be able to cross back."

Holding the end of the cord she'd tied around the shark, Mazur lifted the lid.

"I've tied her just to make sure I can stop her if she goes in the wrong direction. Her bite won't hurt you, much, but we don't want you hurt at all."

All five divers crowded the bin. Nobody said a word.

It took a moment for the little shark to figure out it was free. Then it shot out of the bin in the direction of the abyss. The barrier didn't seem to change or make any sound as she passed it. As soon as she was across, Mazur made a quick motion with her wrist, and the knot in the cord untied.

"The cord is light enough, see? It comes through," she said, reeling it in. "Watch this."

She put the cord in some pocket and pulled out something that looked like a lump of raw fish. She held it up, toward the little shark. "They don't see too well, but she should be able to smell this." She waved it back and forth a little.

The shark caught the scent almost immediately. It flipped itself around and darted back toward them.

And banged into a blank wall.

"Sorry, baby," Mazur said. "Here you go." She pushed the fish morsel so it floated past the barrier. The little shark pounced immediately.

"So," Mazur said. "Safe." The little shark scurried out from them again.

A rat-a-tat screech sounded in Frankie's bones.

"That's our baby," Mazur said. "Calling for her mama. As I said, many of the animals here in the twilight zone use sonar and echolocation methods to move about and communicate. This part of the ocean can actually become very noisy."

Frankie had stopped listening.

Coming up from the depths was a giant shark. Face first. Just like the one in the video. Serrated scar on the snout. Chunk out of the top fin.

The real killer.

All the divers except Mazur, kicked back, paddling furiously until they could overcome their low-brain automatic panic.

The baby shark squealed, another bone-stirring sound. It swam right at the bigger shark, bouncing off its side and rolling over the top of its body. Obviously, right at home.

The mama shark turned away from the fence. She swished her tail hard enough that the divers felt the kick back, and rocketed away. The baby shark, tail swishing furiously followed close behind.

Soon they had both dropped out of sight.

"That's our local monstrush matriarch," said Mazur. "We

believe there are five or six adults in the local pod. This is the first baby we've seen. You all are witness to a once-in-a-lifetime event."

She didn't sound like she was exaggerating for marketing effect. Mazur's whole body was vibrating. Fangirling over a shark.

"The shark population nearby has been thinning. We're trying to help them." Mazur gazed at the pair. "We've tried adding antibiotics modified to work with their genotype. I took a blood sample from our little friend this morning." She looked back at Watike.

"I got it," Watike said. "Put it in the analyzer myself. Should get the data before lunch."

Frankie let herself float closer to the barrier again.

"What other species can we hear?" she asked Mazur. The biologist pressed her hands down in the water, visibly trying to remain calm.

"Many species relying on acoustic signals for communication, navigation, and foraging," she said. "Not a lot at this time of day, but come out for the evening swim, when the day and night animals cross each other, and you can hear plenty."

"Now?" She looked down the barrier toward the VIP guest wing of the resort. "There's a garden down that way with a species of tubformaj rozoj. Tubular roses. When the current passes them, they sound like bells."

Go see the gardens? Frankie looked back at Sansom, who shrugged.

"Why not?" Sansom said over the comm. "I want to see the coral garden over there, too. All last night, looking out from my room, I just wanted to touch it."

"DO NOT touch the coral!" Mazur said. "It's very fragile," she continued in a normal tone. "Get as close as you wish, but don't touch."

"Got it." Sansom nodded to emphasize her understanding.

"Well, I'm not going to look at any coral," Henderson sneered.

"May as well go in. Nothing's ever going to top the monster mama."

"Seriously?" Watike sputtered. "We only just got out here."

Frankie caught Sansom's gaze. She jerked her head. Let's get out of here, she didn't need to say.

The pair swam back to the dining-room dome in happy silence. Unfortunately, the rest of their group was still on the comm.

"You're just mad nobody let you drink this morning."

"Ooooh, that's going to keep me out here longer, babysitting you."

"Friends," Mazur cut in. "Let's head back to the pool. "Once Mr. Henderson is inside, I'll buddy with you."

That must have been agreeable to both, because the snit-snatting stopped.

Past the dining room and another dome and passageway section that must be for staff, they came to the submersible at the end of the guest passageway. It didn't look big enough for five people, let alone twenty.

Sansom must have thought so, too. "If there's really an emergency, I'm running up the tunnel ramp. No way I'm gonna be in a bubble for eight hours with any of these people."

They each checked out their own rooms from the outside. Spike was in a circle on the bed, absolutely crushing Frankie's pillow underneath her. Frankie tap-tapped the glass, not sure if that would even make a sound.

Spike's head shot up, tufted ears pointing straight at Frankie. Frankie waved hello, and then pointed at the foot of the bed. Where Spike should be sleeping.

Spike put her head back on the pillow. She draped her again-scraggly tail over her eyes. They'd need to do another big brushing to get that pelt shiny enough for Spike to become Precious again. Frankie did not look forward to that.

Sansom was heading away from her room, toward the neat rows of coral a ways off. It did look sort of like a labyrinth, a rainbow of blues, greens, reds, purples.

They swam side by side, slow, almost drifting, trying not to disturb the zig-zag schools of minnows. To the side, just past Sansom, a nearly transparent tube fish burst out of the sand and latched onto a minnow nearly as wide as the fish's jaws. They stopped to watch the progress of the minnow down the tube until the fish buried itself again in the sand.

"What do you think of that piggy-back diving style?" Sansom said out of nowhere.

That was the method they had used in the video to abandon that poor girl. Frankie swallowed bile.

"Not my thing," she said.

"But imagine how light you would feel," Sansom pressed. "like you were really one with the sea."

Sure, except for the breathing mask and the wetsuit and the flippers.

"Not worth it," Frankie said. "I need to have hold of my air."

"Right," Sansom said. "Spacer." The word didn't sound nearly so bad in her cheery squeak of a voice. It was nice to hear her happy.

On this side of the resort, the sand wasn't as pure golden white. Here and there, streaks of darker, heavier, sand mixed in.

In one of the darker stretches of sand swayed plants that looked like the pipes of an organ. Tubes tall and short, growing in parallel with one another. These must be the roses.

Frankie touched Sansom's shoulder.

"I'm headed there," she said.

"I'm off," Sansom said, pointing at what must be the main entrance to the coral maze. A touchscreen stood to one side of the wide opening. A ways off-out of photo range—one of those emergency cylinder things stood sentinel. Its somber gray was somewhat dimmed by the yellow buttons of coral that had attached themselves to it.

"Do. Not. Touch the coral," Frankie said.

Sansom laughed.

"Heard it the first time." She veered off, away from Frankie. "Wouldn't dream of it. This place is magic."

As soon as Frankie reached the dark sand patch, she heard a taste of the sounds. But only a taste.

The many-colored tubular roses did, indeed, make music, but she had to go right in among them to hear it. Or at least, hear it above the sound of her own breathing.

Sansom was still at the entrance to the maze, reading something on the screen. Someone who read directions, how nice.

Frankie knelt, careful not to bend any of the meter-high tubes. Marvelous. Thirds and fifths and messier tones, all somehow blending, weaving in and out.

Was the pitch determined by the width of the tubes? Who could say, it was all so dreamy.

Such a delicate melody. Frankie caught herself holding her breath for longer and longer, to hear the sounds' gentle mix.

Which made the scream sound even louder.

Until it choked off.

Chapter Thirteen

At the sound of the all-too-human scream, Frankie propelled herself out of the stand of tubular bells at speed. It warped their dreamy song, bringing her back to sharp attention.

The scream had come over the comms channel, so she didn't have a direction. But the only other person she was responsible for was her diving buddy. Aimee Sansom.

Who was nowhere to be seen.

No one was looking at the information screen over by the entrance to the coral garden maze. Sansom had been there just a minute ago.

Had it been more than a minute? Must have been.

She must have gone in.

Alone

Frankie kicked hard to cover the mere twenty meters between her patch of tube roses and the coral. They were supposed to keep each other in sight.

Or sound.

Frankie tongued her mic on.

"Where are you?"

Nothing.

She reached the entrance, and went in. The first living walls were the same button-style flower coral as had colonized the safety tower outside. Vibrant oranges and blues spread on the shoulder-high walls.

No pale gray diver among them.

She'd reminded Sansom not to touch the coral, right? What else lived among them? Something that scratched? Something that bit?

The colorful corridors led off in three directions. Which to take?

Sound burst into her mask. Sansom had turned her mic back on. She was breathing fast.

"No air," she wheezed. "Only water."

Bloody Safra. The girl couldn't breathe.

Frankie kicked up, out of the maze. Searching would be easier from on high. She should have thought of this before. She should have thought of everything before.

No air. Only water.

Passing the first walls of coral, Frankie saw only more coral and a mess of little fishes. A scary-big sea sponge. A big purple fan-plant, that could be hiding a small gray diver underneath. But wasn't.

This was taking too long.

The light changed, stripes of white-red sliding by. Not her vision clouding, but the emergency lights on the safety tower. Its beacon.

"Look up." Frankie said. "Can you see the red light? Can you get there?"

Stupid question. The woman was in a maze.

"Are you hearing us? Patel? Russo? Mazur? Anyone?" Frankie's scanned the neat paths of sand, all glinting. All empty. "Sansom," she said. "Aimee. Swim up. Up."

Frankie coasted over one of the taller hedges. She was only now nearing the central part. This thing must be more than a hundred meters on the short side. Who would ever make something so big?

On the comm, all she heard was fast breaths, and a soft moan of frustration. Sansom had left the comm open.

Good.

The hedges stepped down toward the center, leaving a large, open area spotted with lumps of coral placed as if they were sculptures. No way Sansom could have gone that far in. Could she?

"Stuck," Sansom whispered. "Red. Bed."

Frankie didn't like the sound of that.

In the walls closing in to the center, the maze gardeners had arranged the colors in palettes of single hues. Frankie darted toward the one that looked the most red.

There, tangled in a thicket of branching coral, was Sansom. Her body thrashed like an eel, trying to break free, but with each struggle, the coral seemed to enfold her more. Her suit was torn all over. She was leaking small droplet chains of red blood from her arms and legs. Skinny little silver fish were diving at the drops.

She was also leaking larger droplets.

Of air.

Frankie dove hard. She tried to come up short just above Sansom, but her gloved hand fell into the coral zone.

The coral, all shades of red from pink to blood, looked deceptively soft and giving. But it wasn't giving up Sansom. The woman's flailing seemed to be drawing her deeper.

Frankie pulled her hand away.

The coral did not let go.

Where were the other divers?

"Help us!" she said on the open comms channel, drifting closer. "Middle of the coral maze, red branching coral patch."

"Can't, breathe." Sansom wasn't looking up, but at the coral. She'd lost one of her diving gloves, which had freed her hand but not her arm.

The thicket wasn't higher than Frankie's thigh, and it wasn't longer than she was tall. How had the woman landed in here? She could have hopped right over it. Close-up, its antler-like branches had rows of tiny hooks, curved and sharp, like cat's claws.

Like that finger-trap game.

Frankie relaxed her trapped hand. It floated free.

Frankie reached for Sansom's leg.

"Aimee, I'm here," she said. "I'm going to touch your leg, at the knee, see? Can you relax it?" Frankie pushed the foot into the coral.

It sprang free.

"Okay, this is going to be hard, but you can do it. Right, Aimee?"

Frankie took the soft sobs she heard as a yes.

"I'm going to push you into the coral. Stay still a sec! That way, when I push you, those hooks in your skin will let go. Like your foot, see?"

Another voice came on the comm. Finally.

"I'm two minutes out," said Monica Valdes. "Stay calm."

Right. And how much air did Sansom have left? This was just like how she'd felt watching everyone die on Wala. Alone. Helpless.

Bullshit. She could do something here, now.

Frankie pushed Sansom's hips in, and out. The woman stopped struggling. She wasn't breathing.

Frankie pushed Sansom's shoulders, chest and arms in, slow.

The girl's whole body came free.

The coral looked as beautiful and innocent as if nothing had ever happened.

Frankie grabbed Sansom by the belt of her dive suit, pushing away some of the tiny vampiric fish that darted in and out and leaned away and down. As soon as the her toes felt sand through the flippers, she bent her knees more.

She kicked hard and up and angled toward the resort. They shot out of the maze. The current was kind, helping push them in the right direction.

Both now vertical and free, Frankie could look into Sansom's masked face. Tears and terror, but she wasn't blue so that was good. Sansom's gaze locked with hers. A thread of hope eeled through all the round panic in her eyes.

Frankie swam back-first toward the resort so she could stay facing Sansom.

"What's your air situation?" she said softly. The spare air tube at the woman's shoulder was the one spewing bubbles. Maybe the main air flow was still good.

"Choked," Sansom said. More tears began to fall.

"We're close, now," Frankie said. "Can you see the bright light, circling, up ahead? That's where more air is." She tried to remember the schematic of the safety station. Outside pocket you could hit to pop the door open, with small air tanks. If not enough, hit the big door, get inside, and hit the green button to pump the water out and more air in. She couldn't remember if there was a control for a second person to start the water-out air-in part from the outside. There must be.

Sansom did not look up. "I see it," she said, looking right at Frankie.

Right. Her suit had a spare air tube.

She let go of Sansom's waist. Her spacer's helmet allowed her to see under her chin, where her back-up tube was clipped on. Frankie unclipped the length from her chin to her shoulder blade.

She held out the end of the tube, near the intake valve on Sansom's regulator.

Sansom took the tube, yanked the bad one out, and plugged the good one onto the valve. Frankie turned the arrow-thing on her spare tank, and air started to flow. Sea water had gotten into the regulator, but Sansom knew how to flush that out.

For a long moment, they just floated, straight and still but for the push of the current. Sansom's breaths, at first raw gulps, started to slow.

Slowly the current spun them, small bobbins in the deep.

The bulk of the resort rolled into Frankie's view, past Sansom's shoulder. They weren't that far from the safety station, but the first dome of the resort wasn't that much farther.

Sansom's eyes had lost that wild look. Something was going right.

They should get moving. First to the station, and see how they felt then. Then, maybe, the domes. But the diving pool was all the way around.

A big fish seemed to be shooting straight at them from between the pilings that held up the resort. Before Frankie could panic again, the form resolved itself into Monica Valdes, swimming fast.

"I see you." Valdes wasn't wearing a dive suit, just a pale one-piece swimsuit that looked silver against the warm blue of her skin. Those enhancements were really working for her, weren't they, Frankie thought wildly.

One of Valdes's arms was stretched out, the other tucked in, fist holding onto the cross-strap of a sack dragging close to her hip. Supplies, probably. She looked like a superhero, flying through the water.

"All breathing?" Valdes said. It was a question, but her voice was calm as a windless sea. "Excellent thinking, to share air. And how much left?"

Frankie hadn't even thought to look. They'd been out here hours.

It must be nearly gone.

She checked her tanks. She'd been out here for not even an hour. She had nearly six hours left, even counting Sansom's usage.

She shook her head, dislodging some of those grabby guppies. It had been a day.

"Plenty."

"Good." Valdes had reached them. She pulled something that looked like first-aid tape out of the bag and wrapped it around the tube and valve of Sansom's rebreather. She tugged on the connection, testing it. Sansom cheeped in surprise.

"Good. This will hold. We need to get you checked out right away. I'm going to pull you both very fast, and I don't want you coming loose."

Valdes took one of Sansom's hands, the right one, the one missing a glove. She turned, and placed Sansom's hand on the back of her shoulder. "Hold here," she said. "Tight as you can. You won't hurt me. Second hand at my hip, grab the fabric."

Frankie mirrored Sansom's position. Valdes turned to look back at her.

"Ready?" In her left hand, Valdes held what looked like a disc from a flying-disc game Frankie used to play at university.

But this one had an engine. It came to life, and the three of them shot toward the resort.

"This toy is called a 'squid jigger,'" Valdes said conversationally as she dodged them through the pylons and into the undercarriage of one of the domes. "Watike named it, of course. It's a little finicky, but when it works it really works.

They made the trip to the pool in less than five minutes.

As they surfaced, Valdes took each of the hands on her shoulders and set them on the edge of the pool. Two pairs of strong hands lifted both Frankie and Sansom up as one. Security chief Patel had Sansom; Jin Watike held Frankie.

They set the two women on their feet, but Sansom immediately sank back to the ground. Frankie followed, not wanting to pull on the air hose no matter how much tape was around it.

She needn't have worried. Sansom had punched the emergency release tabs on her helmet. By the time her rear hit the soft grass, the whole tank-and-mask apparatus fell off her back, onto the short underwater ledge. It would have continued down if Valdes had not caught it.

The resort owner lifted it as if it weighed nothing and handed it to one of the two crew members. She pulled herself gracefully out of the water on the other side of Sansom.

"Let me see your arms," she said softly. She held out a hand, and Watike slapped a waterproofed medical scanner in her palm.

Sansom was not as ready to help.

She scooted away from Valdes, jamming an elbow into Frankie's sternum in the process. Frankie let go the tabs on her own mask and took a pained inhale. Strong hands reached around to continue releasing the tabs.

Sansom shivered.

"You didn't tell me that would happen!" Her shout echoed in the nearly empty dome, as if she'd said it three times.

Valdes winced.

"You said I was safe. Finally," Sansom's voice cracked. Her shivers turned to sobs. "You said."

Valdes's face crumpled in seemingly genuine pain and worry.

"We didn't plan this, Aimee. Absolutely not." Valdes looked close to tears herself. "What happened out there was a freak accident. I am so, so sorry that you had to go through more trauma."

"I have no idea what happened." Now she looked up, at Patel. "No way a piece of coral could have done that much damage."

"It was the snake," Sansom wiped at her nose.

Valdes sighed as if she'd just taken a mountain across her shoulders. "Why a snake? Of all things. That's why we warned you away from the carousel coral. They almost never go in the labyrinth."

"Sea snakes. Nasty."

Watike squatted next to Sansom. She handed the woman a very nice-looking handkerchief.

Then she reached for Frankie's shoulder.

"Your suit seems to have held up remarkably well," Watike said, her tone casual but her gaze intense. "Hers was torn to shreds by the coral, but yours looks practically untouched."

Frankie leaned away from the touch.

"I didn't go near the coral," she said.

"But your hand..." Watike reached for it, but stopped, looking a question at Frankie.

Frankie let her hand be taken.

Three rivulets of blood leaked from what looked like claw scratches.

"Some tearing," Watike said. "But nothing like our suits." She looked at Frankie's face, the tech accenting her eyes whirring. "May I take this, for a bit? Just to study it?"

Frankie couldn't see why not. Until a hiss and a movement at the edge of her vision stopped her as she reached for the clasp to undo her glove.

Spike sat perched on the top of the shelving unit, in the place where the bloody bin had been. The cyvlossic slowly shook her head. No.

Safra's tits. There must be some proprietary folderol in this suit. Blast SystA anyway. Why couldn't they just give her what everyone else got.

Because they want to keep you alive, Frankie heard in Spike's imaginary voice in her head.

"Afraid not," Frankie said to Watike. "This isn't really my suit. So I can't just hand it over to you. I'll ask my friend, who loaned it to me."

"I see." Watike's expression chilled. Then she reconsidered. "You know, I believe that some of Watike Enterprises tech might be included in this suit. Proprietary tech. Not on the market yet." She tapped her chin. "I wonder how that could be."

Watike frowned. "You don't want to cross me. I have a planet's worth of lawyers."

Blasted Safra's tits.

Frankie had no idea what to say to that.

Luckily, Sansom had had enough.

"Stop touching me!" She scrambled to her feet, pushing Watike over in the process. "I can take the shower, rinse, whatever, in my own room."

Frankie scrambled up, too. Spike leapt to the floor, heading for the airlock.

Sansom was still full rant. "Get these flippers off me." She looked up, stomping. "Where's my bathrobe?"

Not a moment later, Patel had both Sansom's and Frankie's robes in her hand. Sansom grabbed them both. She handed Frankie's to her.

"Let's get out of here."

Chapter Fourteen

The antigravity bed in Frankie's room hummed a sweet lullaby, but only Spike, settled into a rather sizeable circle in its center, heard it. In the bathroom, the steady blast of the oversized shower and the bustle of two women taking turns rinsing and stripping off dive suits overran all the resort's efforts at ambient noise.

The guest room had plenty enough cloth towels, and Frankie had a spare extra-large Rusted Fins t-shirt to spare for Aimee Sansom, but the younger woman wrapped herself in her slightly damp robe instead. Her eyes were still a little wild, her breaths quick and shallow.

They checked each other over for cuts and scratches. Sansom had scrubbed her skin with the antibiotic cleansing gel so hard, her arms, back, and legs were striped red.

When Sansom stepped from the bathroom, with its closed walls, into the main room, with its wide ocean view, she froze.

"Could we dim the window?" she said.

"Absolutely," Frankie said. "If we can figure out how."

The control panel was easy to understand, and Frankie made it go dark gray almost immediately. But then she found the menu, with hundreds of choices for backgrounds.

"Ooh, mountains," she said. A range that surely did not exist in this galaxy, a perfect row snow-capped triangles, sprung up.

Sansom stepped into the open space, but scrunched her nose.

"Little chilly."

"Jungle?" Frankie said, changing the view.

A three-times-too-large lion roared at them. They both shrieked.

Spike leapt to attention, head swiveling, looking for the danger. Sansom squeaked a laugh.

"Bloody Safra," Frankie said. "Sorry. I know you don't need any more stress."

"I'm fine," Sansom said. "At least it's not real, you know? Do you have any, I don't know, quiet summer days?"

"Bluster, fog, rain, geez. People want all of this?" Frankie finally got down the menu to Sunny Day. A swath of pale blue appeared on the windows, complete with puffy white clouds slowly drifting.

Sansom also drifted. She tested the rocking of one of the recliners but didn't sit. She settled on her calves on the recliner next to it, but got up immediately. She looked at Frankie's bed.

"Could I pet your kitty?"

Frankie stifled a wince. Spike flicked an ear. She was so, so not a kitty.

But then Spike did the long stretch, beckoning all the pets in the world.

"Precious says yes," Frankie said drily.

Sansom sat at the foot of the bed. As soon as she touched Spike, the cyvlossic rumbled like a cargo truck out of alignment. Sansom slid closer.

"I had to leave my kitty behind," she said. "She's a chocolate chunk, just like your pretty Precious. I'm Aimee, by the way."

Spike rolled on her back, submitting to the adoration with regal grace.

Frankie sat down where Sansom had been, the bed conforming to her weight.

"Evelyn," she said. "How are you doing, really?"

Aimee did not look at Frankie. Her hair swung over her eyes as she bent her head closer to Spike.

"I'm never going diving again," she said. "Never."

Relief washed over Frankie like an on-shore wave. If Aimee stayed out of the ocean, there would be no chance for the nasty shark to eat her. She wouldn't need to be rescued.

She shared a knowing look with Spike, who hadn't stopped purring.

They had succeeded.

With this girl, at least.

Now they needed to shut the pipeline down. Find out who was in on the plan, get all the details they could, tell Bruce and Systems Analysis, and let them handle it. SystA's preferred method was bureaucratic red tape. If that didn't fly, threaten lawsuits. Sneaky spy stuff came third.

So long as the girl was safe.

Aimee stretched out on the bed next to Spike. She tucked her feet inside her fluffy robe and snuggled down.

Frankie let out a long breath. Finally, something worked.

"We'll get you out of this place, safe and sound," she said. "I promise."

Aimee's eyelids were closed, the adrenaline from the day's events finally wearing off. As she sank deeper into the embrace of the bed, the cottony top blanket bunched around her like a cocoon. The blanket pushed Spike away a bit but Aimee didn't seem to notice.

"I don't need another rescue," she murmured, her words slurring together.

Spike stepped softly to the far edge of the bed and hopped down. She headed straight back, to the door to the passageway.

Looking at Aimee, Frankie's mouth tightened. If only the girl knew how much danger she had been in. How few hours away she was from her planned destruction.

Spike scratched softly at the door. Her colleague was right. It wasn't just about avoiding another dive. It was about dismantling the monstrous network that monetized the voyeuristic thrills of the wealthy apex predators of society.

And those folks weren't in this guest room.

Frankie turned away from the sleeping girl. Time to get to work.

Chapter Fifteen

As Frankie approached the executive lounge area from the guest room passageway, Spike's shoulder solid beside her knee, she heard voices, sharp. A tense, hissing exchange that brushed against her ears like static.

Frankie stepped closer to the midnight blue tube wall, staying out of sight, until she reached the round wall of the door panel. She pressed against the narrow space of wall next to the open hatch door. The edge of the shallow cabinet holding emergency equipment dug into her back.

Spike just walked on through.

"Last chance, Henderson," Jin Watike's words were clipped and precise. "Back off, or I'll make sure everyone knows about your little... peccadilloes."

Nathan Henderson's laugh reminded Frankie of their first meeting. Then it sounded mean, now it sounded bitter.

"You spied on me, Watike? With your tiny little drones? We both know that's not admissible in court."

"The court of public opinion holds to different standards," Wattle countered.

"Since when have I ever worried about that?" Henderson scoffed, the tone clear despite the falsetto of his pressure-influenced voice.

Watike must have gotten the message. Frankie heard a huff, and swoosh of fabric. She chanced a glance into the room.

Watike was already at the entrance to the passageway that led to the tech village. She'd changed into a black-on-black pantsuit and restyled her hair after the dive. Her sleek look fought the vibe the rich, organic hues of the resort's interiors were going for. Barefoot, though, she made no sound as she stepped from the grassy carpet to the sandy floor of the passageway. She didn't look back.

Henderson was stretched out in his usual spot, a deep bench of seats near the wall between the dining room and the lounge. Lounging like an emperor amidst the deep aqua cushions, he gazed toward the windows that showed the abyss side of the resort. His drink glass was taller this time, and darker.

Were they partners? Could this be some kind of break up?

Spike padded up to that bank of windows.

"Sweet little Precious," Henderson crooned at Spike. "Where is your pretty, anxious friend?"

That was as good an opening as Frankie was going to get. She rushed into the room as if she'd been worriedly searching for Spike and not standing around casually eavesdropping. Henderson did not look surprised.

"There you are," he said, raising his glass to her and signaling the small servo robot that delivered drinks at the same time. "The great hero. Or is it heroine? Your language baffles me."

He was quoting from an vid drama popular in the last century. Lucky it was a classic in her corner of the system as well, or Frankie wouldn't have caught the reference.

She sat on the edge of the same plush bench Henderson lounged on, sinking a bit into the soft cushioning but not enough for her feet to leave the floor. Spike jumped up to settle in between them. The servo was already back from inside the dining room, carrying a glass matching Henderson's.

"Drink with me?" Henderson said. "It's just punch, with a little extra spice."

Frankie took the glass and held it on her knee.

"I thought I heard you talking to someone," she said. She grimaced inside. So much for subtlety.

"Jin." Henderson raised his glass toward the passageway Watike had gone into. "Our resident mother hen."

"Watike?" Frankie frowned. What would Evelyn say? "She seems a little severe."

"You said it. Accusing me of harassing Monica. As if Monica can't fend for herself." Henderson sighed theatrically. "That woman has more strength in one of those long blue arms of hers than I do in my whole body. Ain't that the truth."

He was drunk. Frankie began to lean even farther away from Henderson, but Spike glared up at her. She settled back down. Spike was right. Sometimes people spilled secrets when they were drunk.

And sometimes they lied.

"Elysium weekend. What a joke. But I shouldn't criticize," he said, glancing at her, trying to leer but not giving it enough oomf. "Did you know that Watike manages to show up for every one of these weekends? Suspicious, if you ask me."

Frankie took a sip of her drink, and stopped. The thing was ten percent juice and ninety percent kick. She winced as it went down.

"Did Valdes tell you that?"

"Monica? Never. I know the old-fashioned way." He pressed

his drink against his forehead, the glass's condensation spreading on his skin. "I use my eyes."

"But doesn't that mean you always show up for them, too?"

"Ah, yes. Wise girl. But look at me. Not a suspect bone in my body."

What was that vid drama again? The one he'd referred to? There was a line about this in there.

"Perhaps you protest too much," she said. Maybe a paraphrase, but the right idea.

"So, you have been listening," he said. He took a slow sip of his drink, the liquid glinting the lounge's soft lighting. "Things go differently underwater, don't you think, room sixteen?" She'd forgotten they were supposed to use room numbers for names.

His icy blue eyes pinned hers, a flicker of challenge. "The pressure changes things. Makes the booze hit harder, stick longer. One of the many charms of the deep."

Frankie nodded, keeping her expression neutral. What was he trying to tell her?

"Looks like you've adapted well to it," she hazarded

Henderson nodded. Correct answer.

"One adapts or drowns, darling."

Outside, the light from the surface was dimming. The schools of tiny silver fish were gone, probably up to a warmer band of water. A patch of those fan ferns had folded in their wide swathes of leaves, hiding the bright yellows and pinks in a layer of gray-green. One of the larger jellyfish was barely visible—not light enough to see clearly but not dark enough that its bioluminescence stood out.

Inside, the ambient music mimicked the sounds Frankie had heard on her swim. Water rushing past, clicks and squeaks and rumbles. And those amazing bells.

Frankie took another tiny sip of her punch, trying to come up with something to bring Henderson back to talking about Watike. But that wasn't who he wanted to talk about.

"She won't say yes, she won't say no," he said, singsong. He held the arm holding his empty glass out straight. The little gray servo must have been hiding behind the arm of the lounge, it popped into action so quick. It took his glass and headed back into the dining room.

He did still have Watike's threat on his mind, but not in the way Frankie wanted. Why ever would Watike care about how close Henderson was to Valdes. What had Watike said?

Harassment. Ah. The love that was unrequited.

Spike huffed in exasperation. Frankie set a hand lightly across Spike's shoulders.

"How many of those have you had?" she said.

Henderson flicked his hand, batting the question away. He turned his head, spearing her with his ice blue gaze.

"It's hopeless, isn't it?"

"You and Monica Valdes?" Frankie hazarded.

Henderson closed his eyes and dropped the back of his head onto the back of the sofa. Its cushioning molded to his nape. Frankie was almost distracted thinking about how this sofa could be constructed, to be so supportive and also so giving. Maybe she just wanted to be distracted. Midlife crushes were so cringe.

"I've given it time," he said. "And space. I've been slow. I've been subtle."

He had not been subtle. At least not this weekend.

Did he really want advice, or just someone to listen? Frankie took another tiny sip of her drink. It did not get less sharp or biting. No ice—the glass itself kept the liquid cool.

He tilted his head to spear her again with those rimy eyes.

"What do you think?"

Sweet Safra's heaven, what did he think she could say about it?

"You've given it time," she said.

"So much time," he sighed.

"You've given her space."

"So much space."

"And…"

"And, nothing. You're right." Henderson thrust himself up, sitting straight. His platinum hair fell perfectly straight. Frankie stared at it. Her hair was probably a rat's nest, even as short as it was now. Brown now, so really looking like a nest.

Henderson rested his elbows on his knees, hands drooping. The servo was back, handing him another tall glass. Henderson took it, and looked at it.

The twilight outside had dimmed to true dark, the water an inky blue-black. Now the bioluminescent creatures swimming past popped out, bodies pulsing their internal radiance. A family of knobby lanternfish drifted, waiting for unsuspecting prey to fall for their tiny tea light of a lure. The sounds must be all different now.

A ghostly white octopus was manipulating something over by the darker coral. Mazur had said during her lecture that morning that the octopus was the only species that the boundary barrier couldn't completely block. The clever creatures had figured out how to stretch themselves narrow enough to fool the sensor-net into thinking they were innocent little fish.

"I've been here long enough," Henderson said. He'd been staring at the glass in his hand. Now he rolled to his feet. He looked down at Frankie, and held out a hand. "Let's get out of here."

"Outside?" Frankie said, leaning back. "Russo recommended only one dive a day."

"Out." Henderson waved at the ceiling. "Up top. You don't want to stay for the show tomorrow, I'm sure of it. Let's scram."

"What? Why me?"

"You can get an aircar. One here. It will come if you call. I've been here so long there's no car for me." All at once, he deflated, dropping back onto the sofa. "No car for me."

Frankie shook her head, trying to keep up. And keep herself out of it.

"You don't need me. Take the car; send it back. Or travel with one of the service trucks. There must be some of those."

"I've been down here so long I'll need a day to decompress, probably. I can't remember. Your car wouldn't get back in time. And the resort transports go way too fast. It'd give me the bends for sure."

Frankie scrambled to remember what the tunnel looked like.

"Could you walk? Take breaks at the turnoffs. No, just take my car."

Spike put both her front paws on Frankie's thigh. They felt like tiny anvils. Frankie looked at her. What was she trying to say?

Not our problem.

"Right," Frankie said. "We'll give you a ride." Spike pounded harder on Frankie's thigh. "But we're not leaving until tomorrow, at the regular time."

"I don't think I can stand to be here one more minute." Henderson all but draped the back of his hand over his forehead. Maudlin midlife infatuation, ugh.

"Go over, pound some on his thigh," Frankie hiss-whispered at Spike.

The resort's outside lights flicked on. They illuminated the flakes of detritus floating down from the upper levels of the water. The sea was so full.

Frankie had downed half her drink when Monica Valdes joined them. Her skin glowed against the fine fabric of her burnt-orange wrap dress. Her face, though, was not as serene as usual. A little tight around the mouth.

Henderson saw her first, as if he had sonar for her musky citrus scent, even through the haze of his aura of bergamot and gin.

"Speak of the devil," he muttered, trying for sarcasm, Frankie thought. But there was no light in his eyes.

Valdes didn't notice or chose to ignore Henderson's comment. She stopped on the other side of Frankie and eyed Spike, who still loafed between Henderson and Frankie. She inclined her head toward Frankie, as if asking for permission to sit next to her. Frankie patted the seat.

Valdes sat as elegantly as she did everything else. Knees together, bare feet crossed and tucked in. She leaned toward Frankie slightly, her sharp-cut hair swinging to her chin.

"Our friend, she is well?"

"Sleeping," Frankie said.

"Not in her room."

Spike lifted her head and gazed at Valdes with interest.

Frankie felt the same way.

"She seemed really mad at you," Frankie said.

Valdes's startling violet eyes bored into Frankie.

"She said something?" the resort owner said. "To you?"

That didn't sound suspicious or anything.

Frankie shrugged. "Just what I overheard at the pool."

Henderson whistled softly. He sounded like those jelly-jaw fishes.

"Monica doesn't like to disappoint anybody."

Valdes stiffened. "I'm responsible for the well-being of all my guests, while they're here." She put a hand on the back of her neck. "I don't like surprises."

"Hence the reliance on Watike surveillance all over the place." Henderson waved at the ceiling near the dining-room entrance. "Like here."

"I know you and Jin are not best friend," Valdes said. "But

there is no doubt that Jin has a rare genius for such systems." She looked at Frankie. "She designed our safety barrier fields and the enhanced surveillance systems that keep this place secure."

The way Valdes said "secure" lingered in the air. Rather a weighted term, with many potential undercurrents.

Was Watike trying to blackmail Valdes, too? Or, from the look of things around here, already been successful at somehow controlling her?

Why? For what?

Murder?

"Sounds like you have quite the setup here," Frankie said. "Must be reassuring, having eyes in so many places."

"It is ... necessary," Valdes said, her gaze drifting, as if seeing beyond the corridor's confines into hidden corners and unseen avenues. "Jin's tech allows me to be everywhere I need to be, overseeing operations and ensuring guest safety."

A necessity but not a welcome one?

"And Watike? What does she get out of it?"

Valdes gave her another of those unsettlingly direct stares.

"Power. Jin is ... complex. Her motivations are often layered."

She seemed to hear something Frankie didn't. She rose and started walking toward the passageway to the guest rooms.

Spike immediately hopped off the bench. Heading for the passageway.

By the time Aimee Sansom appeared in the entry, Spike stood between Valdes and the younger woman.

Aimee, surprisingly alert and poised, was back in her own clothes, a basic tie-dyed tunic over black footless tights and flip-flop sandals. She clutched her still damp wetsuit against her chest.

Her auburned hair clipping her jawline, framing a face that lacked its earlier chronic trepidation. With purpose in her stride, Aimee appeared renewed.

She walked right past Valdes as if she hadn't seen the woman.

"Evie, thanks. That was just what I needed." She did not look out the windows but toward the passageway to the tech village and, farther on, the diving pool. "I'm going to take my suit back. I want to talk with Samir about what happened."

Monica Valdes approached them. She tapped the lobe of her ear, one of the usual methods for opening up an implanted communications channel.

"You're right," she said to Aimee's back. "Samir is at the pool. I can take you."

Aimee didn't turn around.

"I know the way. I want to talk to Samir. Alone."

Valdes knew when to back off, but she didn't have to like it.

Spike had followed her, and now brushed Aimee's knee. The cyvlossic gave Frankie a hard stare.

Frankie jumped up.

"Right. I was headed that way myself." She rolled to her feet. Before she could think where to put her half-finished drink, the little servo robot was back to take it from her.

"I would have taken yours back too," Aimee said as they walked together toward the passage. "But it wasn't there."

What? She'd left it hanging over the back of one of the loungers, with a towel underneath.

"What?" Aimee stopped and turned. Frankie had stopped walking. "You took it back already, right?"

Spike growled.

Watike. She'd been fascinated by Frankie's suit. Hungry for it.

But how would she have gotten into Frankie's private room? Especially with a sleeping Aimee inside.

Of course.

Watike built the security system. She only had to tell the door to open, and send a cleaning servo to pick it up. The servo probably rolled right past, her suit in its little square belly, while Frankie was sitting daydreaming the afternoon away.

Time to visit the resident tech genius.

Frankie took a deep breath, forcing herself to focus on the task at hand. She turned to Aimee, a warm smile spreading across her face.

"Sorry. I had a thought. I've got something to do right now, but how about we meet up in a couple hours? Have dinner together?"

Aimee hesitated for a moment, her pale skin flushing slightly at the invitation.

"I know a great place," Frankie said, keeping her tone light.

That made Aimee laugh.

"Sure," she said. They'd reached the turnoff for the main dome of the tech village. "That'll give me three whole hours to primp. Later."

With a wave, she continued straight, her wet suit slung over her shoulder like a trophy.

Frankie's gaze turned to the short tube ahead of her. Her steps slowed.

How best to approach a tech genius who seemed to hold a lot of secrets—and had a penchant for full-cover surveillance?

Spike head-butted her in the back of the knee.

"One step at a time," she chirped, and then stopped, surprised.

The pressure must be getting to her voice box, too.

Chapter Sixteen

The main dome of the Research and Innovation Village was the first place in the Valdes Underwater Resort where Frankie didn't hear any ambient music or water sounds. Just the whirrs and clicks of machines, and the soft chimes of itty-bitty autonomous tractors backing up.

She and Spike strode past the outer edge of the village, paying no mind to the soft glows of the holographic displays that were projecting ever-developing data from various experiments and simulations. They avoided the modular workstations, each wide enough for the various remote- and self-controlled servos to operate in. Most of the humans who worked in the village lived up-top, directing avatars and robots through the various experiments and stress tests down here. Certainly easier on the body that way.

The air in the facility was warmer, carrying the metallic tang of freshly machined components and the faint sting of solvents. The floor beneath their feet, mocha-colored hexagon tiles, looked smooth but felt pocked. No one was going to slip in here.

They couldn't help slowing when they reached the center of the dome. A clear cylindrical aquarium as wide as a hug stretched from floor almost to ceiling. Amid the treelike green plants swaying inside swam the tiniest little sharks.

Frankie had to step closer. How old were these things? She touched the wall of the tank with the tip of a finger, just in front of one of the miniature monsters.

It lunged at her, tiny baby teeth out.

Frankie yanked her hand away. So much for interspecies harmony.

Frankie turned her back on the nasty baby and scanned the circle of the room. She found Watike on the far side, alone, in an area with wet-lab tables. The inventor looked like she was stuck inside in a geodesic cube made of light.

As they got closer, the light resolved into a series of branches and acronyms. A 3D model of some advanced surveillance network? The resort itself?

Watike did something twisty with her hand, and a small branch of the model rearranged itself. Some of the bands connecting the acronym spheres were thin, others double or triple thickness.

A synthetic compound, then. Super complex.

For a moment, Frankie just watched. Spike pushed at her, but she didn't want to interrupt. Watike was completely engrossed, her fingers dancing through the air with a precision and decisiveness that spoke of years of experience.

Then as if a circuit had switched open, she stopped. She looked up, her dark eyes glittering inside their shiny implanted frames with a mixture of annoyance and curiosity.

"Did we have an appointment?"

"What is that?" Frankie stepped closer, past a couple ceramic worktables and almost to the edge of the hologram.

Watike swept her arm across and down. The image vanished.

"Nothing. Just a project for Mazur. Now she's worried that the sharks have some wasting disease. They look chunky enough to me."

"A vitamin?"

Watike tilted her head, as if she was trying to analyze the structure of Frankie's head using only her augmented eyes. Her black bodysuit hugged her lean frame, including her stiff, crossed arms.

"A vaccine. Ugh. Don't let that animal any further into my lab."

Spike, at Frankie's side, looked around the room coolly. Then she leapt onto the nearest ceramic table. Watike huffed, clearly irritated. Spike sprawled onto her back, and started licking one of her rear paws.

The table started to talk.

"That parameter is not available," it said in Watike's voice but nicer.

Spike must have turned on a screen with the touch of her paw. Or her butt.

"Cloner off," the real Watike said, sharp. "What do you want? Wait, did Henderson send you? That ass."

Frankie would not be distracted.

"My dive suit. I know you have it."

"Oh, your suit." Watike waved a hand dismissively. She walked to one of the ceramic tables that had scopes and other equipment on it.

Frankie glared at Spike. <u>Stay there</u>.

Spike slowly licked a path up the back of her leg, staring at Frankie the whole time.

"It's a fake," Watike said. "You were taken."

"Excuse me?"

Watike waved Frankie over to the table.

"Look." She touched a magnifying scope and a screen popped into view in front of them. "Just a paint job. Underneath it's the same suit as all the rest of us. Good suit, mind, but not special. Hope you didn't pay too dearly for it."

Frankie did not have time to wonder why SystA would have painted her dive suit.

"But the fact remains. You took it. Without permission."

"Nonsense," Watike said smoothly. "I was nowhere near your room. I can show you the camera data if you want."

Frankie was sure the woman could, doctored and undoctored.

Watike looked past the scope, at a bank of three square little servo carts, basically open wagons with four arms tucked in.

"If I had to guess, I'd say a cleaning servo came in for its daily inspection, and carted off the suit back to the diving pool. That's where they should be, right?"

Frankie just bet.

"So why is it here, then?"

Watike's arms went wide.

"Who can say?"

Enough of this. The suit wasn't the puzzle. Well, it was, or it was its own puzzle, or something. Frankie shook her head. And froze.

Spike wasn't on the table any more.

Watike must not have noticed. She was still smirking. Time to divert attention. Nothing for it but to be direct.

"We know you have every bit of this resort surveilled. Is it really just to test new tech?"

Watike smiled, a thin stretch of lips that didn't reach her knowing eyes. "Knowledge. It's priceless. In the right hands, it commands everything else—safety, power, control."

"Like you are trying to control Nathan Henderson?"

"Oh, him. I'm so sick of his puppy eyes at Monica. He's so thick, for such a slimy sort. She's so not interested."

Watike's gaze flicked away from Frankie, wistful.

It might not be Henderson alone who held an unrequited torch for Monica Valdes.

Frankie swallowed her fledgling sense of empathy. She would not be distracted. Not even by Spike, creeping up on Watike from behind.

"We know all about your surveillance tech," Frankie said.

"Of course you do. 'We,' indeed," said Watike. "I'm not the only one sending ELF-band transmissions here and there. What are you and your friends doing? Where are your friends, anyway?"

Spike came up short, surprised. Frankie kept her face still and her topic front of mind.

"The data gathering," she plowed on. "The interest in the resort's shark population. Genetically modified sharks, Dr. Mazur says." Frankie took a breath. "We think it's connected to the deaths that have happened here."

Watike's eyes widened, genuine shock on her face. "Deaths? What deaths?" She grabbed Frankie's wrist. "Did that poor girl die? I thought she just got scraped up."

Frankie's reeled, taken aback by Jin's reaction. It read as sincere. She had been so sure that Watike was involved somehow, but the tech genius seemed genuinely confused by the accusation.

"I know that several guests have died here under mysterious circumstances," Frankie pressed on, studying Watike's face for any sign of deception. "And your technology, your methods... You would have seen it all. Don't deny it."

Spike pushed Watike hard at the back of the knees. The woman didn't seem to notice. She shook her head vehemently.

"Deaths? Saints, no, you've got it all wrong." Watike's breaths were so fast she sounded like she'd been running. "Yes, I've been testing my surveillance improvements here, and yes I've been gathering data, and maybe some of it has been a little corporate espionage. You would not believe who comes to these kinds of resorts."

She shuddered, and squeezed herself tighter. "But it's all for the sake of the science. Of innovation. I would never be a part of anything that would harm anyone. We don't even license our work to make weapons."

As Spike silently circled their feet, Frankie frowned.

Safra's blasted butt.

Everyone at this resort was reading as kind. Not a killer among them.

Everyone was lying. Had to be.

Something didn't add up. Or she wasn't smart enough to see how it did.

No matter. She'd feel like the incompetent detective later. The important part was that Aimee was safe. SystA would have another three or four months to break the case before anyone else would be in danger.

She bent to pretend to pet Spike.

"Clear?" she said subvocally. Did Spike think Watike was clean, too?

"Mmm-hmm." Yes.

Safra's blasted ass.

Watike swept up a pile of gray fabric and dumped it into Frankie's arms almost before Frankie was on her feet again.

"Take it. Fake suit." She shook her head, still seeming distracted. "I melted the small lacerations on your glove back together," she said. "No high tech needed."

As Frankie turned to go, Watike grabbed her arm.

"Listen. Nobody is going to die at this resort. Monica wouldn't let them."

But somebody had died here already. More than one body.

126

Spike stomped in front of her toward the passageway back to the VIP area.

Bewildered, carrying her dive suit in her arms as she left the research village, Frankie could have sworn it weighed twice as much as before.

Chapter Seventeen

Frankie decided to wear both the sunset rose silk dress and the gorgeous night-ocean velvet bolero jacket. This dinner was a celebration, after all.

Then why didn't it feel like one?

Aimee wasn't in the lounge outside the dining room when Frankie and Spike arrived. Frankie went to the window looking over the abyss. Ha ha, no food for you tomorrow.

A white octopus kept popping its head above the rim of the chasm and then down. Playing with a friend?

Then she saw Spike bobbing her head up and down, much like the octopus. Could the octopus see that far? Apparently so—when Spike did a fake-out, dipping but popping right back up again, the white guy outside flashed pink for a moment.

It was hard to see much else. The outside lights had been tilted to aim their beams almost horizontally. Looking for something besides sharks, apparently.

Frankie refocused her eyes, turning the window into a mirror. In the room behind her, she saw Nathan Henderson, of course, on his favorite sofa, but also Jin Watike speaking with Samir Russo and Sylvana Patel. Looked like the second seating was going to be mostly staff.

Frankie sighed.

"A punch-soaked would-be Romeo. A techie who refuses to sell her work to the military." They'd messaged SystA when they got back to their room after talking with Watike. Within an hour, Bruce had messaged confirming Watike's peaceful tendencies.

"A diving guide who hasn't been here for every event. A security chief who hadn't been here two months yet.

"We're running out of suspects."

She was missing something, she was sure of it. Something obvious. But then, so was Spike. What could possibly fool them both?

Or who.

It was time to take another look at Monica Valdes.

Frankie saw Aimee's reflection hurrying toward her. Lovely in a forest green caftan and matching turban, the woman looked as if the weight of the world had been lifted off her neck. But her eyes still darted here and there.

Frankie turned around and smiled.

"Thanks for waiting," Aimee said. "All the couples usually take the first seating, and they all stare and stare at me. Or they stare at me while pretending not to. It's like they've never seen a young person before."

"Maybe they're vampires," Frankie said.

"That little lady always in gray must be. I swear, she salivates when she sees me." Aimee shuddered theatrically. The smile that followed was genuine.

"Well, it's only us two, looks like," Frankie said. "And the entire resort crew."

"Really?" Aimee turned to look. "Guess no one is night diving, then. Why would you even come here, if not to get out in the water?"

Interesting thought, from someone who almost suffocated underwater this very day.

"I saw the gray lady leave earlier. She frowned at Precious, here. We're trying to stay way out of her way. She's allergic. I even washed Precious special with the anti-dander shampoo."

Aimee squatted down to Spike's level. She held out a hand for the cyvlossic to sniff. "Bet that went over well." Spike consented to be petted. "But feel how silky and glossy you are now."

One of the burgundy-suited servers appeared at Aimee's side. Spike followed them to the entrance and then veered off to perch on the warm spot that Henderson had left on the sofa by the wall.

The server sat them at the table Aimee had had the night before: front window center. Easy to see why the woman wouldn't want a repeat of last night. She must have felt like a store display in holiday season.

The server poured them a small flute of sparkling white wine.

Aimee raised her glass in a toast.

"To the brightest future!" she said.

Frankie clinked to that.

Samir Russo's generous laugh sounded behind Frankie. Aimee looked toward the sound.

"Guess what?" she said. "I'm going diving with you all tomorrow."

"What!" Frankie, aghast, nearly jumped to out of her seat. She saw Spike streak into the entryway, ears alert.

"I know! I know!" Aimee's grinned. "Isn't it great? After today's debacle, I thought, no, never again. But then I dropped off my suit, you know, this afternoon. And I talked with Samir about it. He explained how amazingly rare something like that happens. And I was still like, yeah. right."

No way she was going in the water tomorrow. Frankie had to make sure of it.

"And rightly so," Frankie started, but Aimee rolled right over her words.

"But then he started to convince me. And he's right, you know, if I don't get in the water right away, I'll stay scared. And then I'll never get in again."

Frankie was going to kill Samir Russo. Who was he to give reasonable-sounding advice at a time like this?

"Sure," Frankie got in quickly. "But not tomorrow."

Aimee seemed to notice that Frankie wasn't quite as delighted as she was.

"Why not tomorrow?" She said, a slight frown starting to creep into her sunshine. "After all, we're leaving after that."

"What about your air," Frankie said, scrambling for something that would sound reasonable to a young person who still thought they were invincible.

"What about my air?"

Got it. Frankie leaned forward, locking eyes with Aimee. Trying to look concerned but not panicked.

"Your body went through a traumatic experience. You were deprived of oxygen for some time, which can have serious consequences. Your lungs and respiratory system need time to fully recover."

It was working. The frown was gaining ground over Aimee's giddy grin.

"Pushing yourself too hard too soon could lead to trouble. Like pulmonary edema or even a pneumothorax. Those are nothing to take lightly."

The server returned, to refill their glasses. Frankie reached across and placed a hand on Aimee's arm. Focus. Reel the girl in.

"I know you want to get back in the water right away to overcome your fear. It's a smart idea. But diving here is tough. Please listen to your body-it needs rest."

"Pah." Aimee held up her glass again. "No time like the present."

Frankie was going to destroy Samir Russo.

Their first course arrived, another cold soup that would taste like mist. Aimee lifted her spoon to taste it, and then set the spoon down.

"I thought you would be excited for me," she said. "You're just like all the rest. Never letting me make my own decisions."

What?

"Don't look so shocked," Aimee sneered. "I know how you people are. Sure, we're friends, but only so far as I do what you say."

"It's nothing like that!" Frankie could not believe this was happening. "You know what?"

She stopped.

"What?" Aimee said despite herself.

Frankie struggled with her brain for something, anything.

Yes.

"Let's stay on another day. I'll pay. Dive on Monday, when we're sure your lungs are clear."

That would work. Frankie started to breathe again.

Aimee stood up so fast she knocked her chair to the floor.

"Who are you? You're working for my mother, aren't you?" Aimee looked around wildly. Her face had gone blotchy red.

What? Frankie looked at Spike. What was happening?

Suddenly, Monica Valdes was at their table, taking Aimee's arm, turning to lead her away. But before they moved, Valdes looked back at Frankie.

"Sit down. You stay away from her."

"No!" Frankie was desperate now. "Something terrible is going to happen to her tomorrow. I just know it! I can see it!"

"Where is your animal?" Valdes said. Frankie looked to the entryway. Valdes followed her gaze. "Let it in," she said to the server. "She's overwrought. Precious will comfort her."

"I'll be right back," Valdes said.

That sounded like a threat.

Chapter Eighteen

As Monica Valdes led a visibly shaken Aimee away from the dining room, Frankie felt the world tilt beneath her feet. The accusation hung in the air, a sandbag as big as a table pressing down on her shoulders.

Spike pawed at her leg, and made her painfully scratchy version of a meow. Frankie pushed her palms into Spikes warm tufts of fur.

"What just happened?" she whispered.

Her mind raced, trying to make sense of the sudden shift in Aimee's demeanor. The pieces of the puzzle of this whole assignment seemed to scatter and rearrange themselves in ever creepier patterns.

Aimee's words echoed in her mind. Who are you?

Frankie sat back up. The dainty cup of mist-soup still sat on the table in front of her. She didn't even pick up the tiny spoon, but the cup itself. She downed it in one swallow.

Spike head-butted Frankie's other hand. She stroked Spike's head, more to soothe herself than the cyvlossic.

Aimee. Frankie frowned, parsing through their conversations.

Aimee had never spoken of her family, but the rules of this weekend were not to pry. Frankie had assumed her reticence stemmed from a desire for privacy, but what if there was more to it?

Could there be more to Aimee's past than SystA had uncovered? The thought of Aimee's mother being somehow involved in the deaths at the resort sent a chill down Frankie's spine.

When the next course arrived, something with fish and cayenne sauce, she couldn't stomach it. She asked for another cup of the mist-soup instead.

Aimee's mother? It seemed far-fetched, but no more so than a woman pretending her cat wasn't a sentient being smarter than she was herself.

Frankie glanced at Spike.

"What did I miss?"

Spike shook her head slightly. She rested her cheek on Frankie's thigh.

Questions tangled themselves in her mind. How had Aimee been chosen this week's victim in the first place? Had her family paid to have her killed, as part of some twisted, elaborate scheme? Bruce had told her SystA had been hired by the grieving families of women who had died at the resort. But were they truly grieving, or were their tears nothing more than a façade?

How could people even think that way? How could she?

No. She didn't believe it. The families were clean. They had to be.

Frankie was so lost in her thoughts that she barely registered when Monica Valdes returned. The resort owner sat in the chair Aimee has vacated, body rigid, face frosty, eyes sharp and accusatory. But as she took in Frankie's genuine distress, her expression softened slightly.

"I don't even know who Aimee's mother is," Frankie said, her voice barely above a whisper. "All I want is to help, to protect Aimee. That's it."

Valdes studied her for a long moment, as if weighing the sincerity of her words. Finally, she stood again.

"If you would follow me," she said, her tone leaving no room for argument.

Spike followed Valdes immediately. Halfway across the dining room, the cyvlossic looked back. Get up, her expression said.

Frankie followed them through the many winding corridors of the resort, the soft glow of the bioluminescent walls casting eerie shadows on their faces.

Valdes led them to a nondescript door, which slid open with a soft hiss to reveal an office that looked like it had been lifted from the tech village.

The room hummed in the key of electricity. And it was dry; Frankie wished she'd finished her drink from before. The floor had the same looks-smooth-but-not tiles. The desktops were ceramic and waist high. The stools nearby were not padded.

The room was bathed in the cool blue light of multiple holographic displays, each showing a different area of the resort. Frankie's eyes widened as she realized the true extent of the surveillance system.

"Every part of the resort is on-camera," Valdes said, her fingers dancing across a floating screen that must be a control panel. "Jin Watike is a genius. And now a silent partner in the resort. We plan to expand."

Valdes brought up a recording on one of the larger screens, showing a clumsy swimmer in diving gear—a guest—in distress. Apparently caught in a dangerous current, they were being pulled away from the safety of the resort. Whoosh, they swooped past the poles that marked where the resort's invisible barrier stretched.

Spike jumped on a stool next to the screen to see better.

Frankie watched, transfixed, as the scene unfolded. But at the moment the guest was in the greatest peril, she couldn't help but wince, closing her eyes against the surge of empathy and fear.

Valdes must have seen her reaction.

"Don't worry," she said, her voice so soothing. "Look."

Frankie still waited another few seconds. When she next looked at the image, the guest was encased in some kind of shimmering net, a net made of something that allowed it to be towed back through the barrier into safer waters.

"That's the closest we've ever come to losing anyone. He was hurt even less than poor Aimee today." Valdes touched her chest near her heart for a moment, remembering.

"So you see, there's no need to worry," she said. "None at all."

Spike's head tilted, looking at the screen as the rescue sequence began again.

Valdes took Frankie's hand. It was a contest whose was colder.

"We haven't lost anyone yet," she said.

The words hung in the air, heavy with implication. Frankie's gaze snapped to hers, eyes wide with uncertainty.

"But you have," she said softly, wonderingly.

Valdes's perfectly serene face, even more blue in the light from the electronics, froze. Cracks started to form—a slow blink of the eyes, a tic of a twitch at the corner of her mouth.

The resort owner had slipped.

The next instant, Valdes's demeanor flipped. She drew herself up to her full height, her eyes flashing with anger.

"I know who you are," her voice colder than the abyss. "Jin figured it out this afternoon.

Frankie looked at Spike. Which 'you' was Valdes talking about? The cargo pilot? The child orphan of Wala? The really bad spy?

"You're a spy, aren't you?" Valdes bit out. "You're working

with one of those gossip rags. Looking for a lurid story. Peccadilloes of the rich and famous."

Frankie opened her mouth to protest, but Valdes cut her off with a sharp gesture. "You'll get nothing from us here," she said.

She swiped her arm down, like a scythe through grass. "Nothing. And don't forget, you signed a nondisclosure agreement and all our other legal form. If you say one word about us, I'll destroy you."

With a few quick taps on her screen, Valdes sealed Frankie's fate.

"I've arranged for the car to pick you up at six am tomorrow," she said. "I want you and your cyvlossic—a cyvlossic! here!—out of my resort before any of the other guests are up. Tomorrow is a big day for them. And nothing is going to spoil it."

Chapter Nineteen

Frankie stumbled out of the security office, bewildered and desperate. The eerie emptiness of the resort haunted her as she stepped from one dimly blue-lit passage to the next. Aimless, she let her feet guide her through the locked puzzle of passageways and domes.

How had everything gone so wrong?

Just this afternoon, they were riding high. Aimee was safe, tucked inside the resort for the rest of the weekend. Frankie and Spike had time to work the side project of fact-finding for SystA's lawyers. They were going to shut the whole "Elysium Weekend" thing down.

Now, Aimee was in imminent danger—just hours away from the dive that would kill her. Frankie had no idea how to stop it. And she and Spike wouldn't even be here to try, getting booted out of the resort before daylight.

Through the main dome of the tech village, Frankie's footsteps echoed on the textured composite floor, the sound amplified by the oppressive quiet of the sleeping resort. Even the servos were sleeping.

The air was cooler and carried less of the usual daytime scents. The brine tang of the ocean that surrounded them bullied its way forward.

Beside her, Spike padded along, her presence suggesting a comforting warmth from the chill. But she didn't come near enough to touch, and so offered none.

Frankie's mind raced as she walked, replaying the events of the past few hours in an endless, tormenting loop. The accusations, Aimee's hurt expression, the sickening moment when Frankie realized all her plans had foundered.

She slid on by the corridor leading to the VIP area. She did not want to even catch a glimpse of the abyss beyond its windows. That ruled out returning to her room, as well.

Instead, they circled back, through the mocking shadows left by the bioluminescent night lights.

She found herself in the empty reception area. Its fake-sand floor didn't seem to welcome her steps now.

Frankie stopped at the back of the dome, close to the transparent floor-to-ceiling wall. Only two spotlights criss-crossed the expanse, dim slices that most of the dark-water animals avoided. Spike settled beside her, finally offering a bit of warmth.

She pressed her hands against the thick, chilled glass, its smooth surface doing nothing to calm the emotions storming inside her. Outside, puffy bug-eyed fish and thick jelly squid things paid no attention to her at all.

Outside, this weekend, a young woman would die.

Frankie had watched people die before, millions of them. But she'd seen the destruction from orbit. No bodies visible from four hundred-plus kilometers away. It was different when the body was right in front of you. When you've touched it. Helped take air tanks off its back.

This was so different. Worse, in a way. At least she hadn't had any idea that her home planet was about to collapse. She wasn't dreading it.

Frankie set her fingertips on the window. Reaching for something. What? Forgiveness from the lantern fish? Good luck.

Gazing blindly at the inky depths, she replayed again every moment since she'd watched that first video, back in her tiny, comfortable apartment.

She was having trouble seeing.

And she certainly didn't hear Monica Valdes approach, didn't sense her presence until the resort owner spoke.

Even Spike startled.

"Jin didn't believe it, but I knew it was you," Valdes said, her voice soft but filled with a quiet intensity. "Child Orphan of Wala. You still stand the same way. Hips forward, hands locked, looking so far into the distance. You still cry the same way. Silent. Your face so carefully quiet, locked down so far."

Another cover blown. Frankie's heart deflated even further. She wasn't often recognized, these days. It never went well.

"What I couldn't figure out was why you were here," Valdes continued, her steps coming closer. Frankie could see her movements in the window's reflection now. "What could possibly entice a woman who had seen so much death to our little Elysium Weekend?"

Frankie didn't turn. Her tears did not stop flowing.

"You're a killer. Murderer."

"You don't know what you're talking about." Valdes passed behind Frankie, brushing her back with a shoulder. "No. You would never have come to an Elysium Weekend on your own initiative. Whose family hired you?"

She'd finally hit on the truth. This time, her accusation broke something inside Frankie. She had nothing to lose now but the weight of all Evelyn's pretending.

"I've seen the video footage," Frankie said, not looking at her, not even in the window's reflection "I know what you've done."

Valdes didn't react. "You never have," she said.

Frankie's mind raced, desperately trying to make Valdes see. "Ask Spike," she blurted out, grasping at straws.

Valdes raised an eyebrow. "Spike?"

"Precious, I mean." Frankie cursed herself inwardly. She was failing at everything, even remembering her own partner's alias.

Valdes was silent. Frankie chanced a glance at her.

Valdes must have seen something new. A flicker of understanding passed across her face.

"Ahhh," she said. "I think I see. You watched a pirated video, and you think you saw the truth."

Frankie's tears stopped abruptly. Confusion and disbelief warred in her thoughts. How could it not be the truth?

"What?"

Valdes gestured for Frankie to follow her.

"Come with me," she said, her tone gentle now, but insistent. "Please."

Frankie turned away from the reception area's window. Now what did Monica Valdes want to do to her?

Spike was already in front of Valdes, heading for the offices, ready to find out what the resort owner thought so important now. Frankie didn't know if she could handle any more revelations. She felt raw.

But Valdes probably wasn't going to kill her, now that she knew Frankie would be missed. And Frankie had survived worse than anything else Valdes had in store for her.

She allowed herself to be led away from the reception area.

They stepped back into the resort's surveillance room. But they didn't stop there.

Valdes pressed the wall at the back of the room. A door slid open.

The office beyond was nothing like the surveillance chamber. A perfect blend of elegance and technology, the warm, organic colors of the resort's aesthetic seamlessly integrated with sleek, modern elements.

A large, curved white-oak desk dominated the center of the room, its surface a glossy brown that reflected the warm vanilla lights set into the ceiling. One wall was lined with bookshelves, each with glass doors that locked. A scattering of cloth-bound books shared space with crystal sculptures, folded-paper bird, and a menagerie of small stuffed land animals.

But it was the far wall that drew Frankie's attention. It was nearly covered by a vast tapestry, made of threads both fine and rough. Every part so detailed, it seemed to be dancing on the wall. As she stepped closer, Frankie recognized the resort, seen as if in a dream or vision.

At the center of the dream, woven in shimmering, iridescent thread, was a portrait of Monica Valdes herself. But it was not the distant, congenial figure Frankie knew. This Valdes was smiling, her violet eyes brimming with warmth and compassion, her hands outstretched as if waiting to hug you tight.

Frankie's eyes drifted away from the so-intricate tapestry, her mind a maelstrom of confusion. Nothing made sense anymore. The woman depicted in the tapestry, the woman standing before her now, seemed a galaxy away from the calculating killer she would have to be to run such a murder scheme as Elysium Weekend.

Valdes gestured for Frankie to sit in one of the green plush, overstuffed armchairs in front of the desk. As she sank into the soft, supple fabric, wide enough for Spike to come up and sit beside her, Frankie felt a momentary sense of ease.

It didn't last.

Valdes sat in the other armchair, her movements graceful and purposeful. She waved a hand, pulling up a screen that she set between them.

"These are files that are not kept any network," she said. "Only one copy. Only here."

With a few deft movements, Valdes pulled up two videos and placed the images side by side. When Frankie recognized the scene, Frankie's heart seized. It was the girl she had seen in the video SystA had shown her, the one that no one had been able to save.

Frankie felt bile rise in her throat. She started to push herself up from the chair, ready to flee the room, the resort, this entire wretched planet. But before she could get moving, Spike was on her lap.

They were staying.

Valdes was watching her, compassion and worry lining the sides of her eyes.

"Fridrika," she said. Frankie hadn't heard her own name in months. "You have to promise to watch. Just once. Every frame."

Frankie squeezed her eyes shut.

Valdes persisted. "I saw you do that when I played the earlier clip." Spike chirruped, surprised. "I need you to watch."

With a shaky nod, Frankie sank back into the chair, her hands gripping the armrests like a lifeline.

"Do it," Spike chirped.

Valdes started the videos. They showed the same event; one from the familiar view, from the dining room window. The other camera must have been attached to the cliffside of the abyss.

The girl in the bikini, her face a mask of terror. The monstrous shark, rising from the deep like a nightmare made flesh. So many razor-sharp teeth.

Excruciating.

At the crucial moment, Frankie's eyes slammed shut, her breath coming in sharp, ragged gasps. She felt a gentle touch on her arm and opened her eyes to see Valdes leaning across the screen, her expression soft and understanding.

"Just look," she said, her voice a soothing balm to Frankie's frayed nerves. "Hold onto your friend." She looked at Spike.

Frankie took a deep, shuddering breath, grabbed Spike so tight the cyvlossic yelped, and opened her eyes.

Valdes advanced the videos slowly, frame by painstaking frame, narrating the events.

"The girl looks like she is being sucked sideways into the shark's mouth—as if the shark is inhaling strongly and sucking her in. But see?" She traced the path of the girl's movement. "It isn't. She is swimming into it, of her own volition."

Spike stiffened, curiosity piqued. Frankie frowned, and leaned forward. The girl's face still read as terrified. She kicked and struggled.

And put herself into the jaws of the monster.

In the cliffside view, a pair of divers appeared at the bottom of the frame, well out of view of the forward camera's view. Rising from the depths like guardian angels.

As soon as the girl is near its mouth, the shark thrashes, which somehow causes it to drop briefly out of front-camera view.

On the cliffside camera, a diver pulls the girl free of the shark's mouth. No blood, no terrified face. The second diver has a girl-sized piece of meat clad in something like skin and a mockery of a bikini They push it to the waiting shark. The shark chomps down on the fake girl and starts to thrash. Not two seconds pass before it is in view view of the first camera, busily mauling its fake-girl snack.

Fake girls. Frankie leaned back in the chair, stunned.

"These sharks," Valdes said, answering the unspoken query. "They're sentient. They work with us, they do this piece of acting, in exchange for food and the preservation of their territory."

"And vaccines," Frankie said wonderingly.

"And, we hope, soon, vaccines." Valdes leaned back in her chair, her fingers interlocked beneath her chin.

"These young women, the ones you thought were being sacrificed? They're not victims. They're survivors. We're giving them a chance at a new life, released from the horrors of their past."

"Our little witness-protection program," Valdes said with satisfaction. She shot Spike a look. "If you want to investigate someone, take a look at these families.

Fresh tears sprang to Frankie's eyes. Relief, such sweet relief. Before she could stop herself, she swept Spike up into a big hug.

This once, Spike put up with it.

Chapter Twenty

Spike struggled out of Frankie's grasp after less than a minute. Enough hugging, the raised tufts of fur on her back said. She jumped lightly from the overstuffed chair onto the woven-grass flooring of Monica Valdes's private office. Tall tail up, she turned to look at Frankie.

Time to go.

But Frankie didn't have all the answers yet.

What had started Valdes on this very dangerous, weirdly specific method of rescue? Surely there were safer ways to disappear people who wanted to disappear.

But the woman looked as tired as Frankie felt. Her posture in the chair sagged, leaning to the far side. She rested her head on her propped-up hand. Her beautiful, enhanced eyes drooped.

She'd probably also missed dinner. Next time, Frankie was going to wait to set her dining partner off until after the main course.

"Thank you for showing me this," Frankie said, standing.

"Call me Monica." Valdes didn't rise. "We can talk more in the morning. I know you have questions." Even her chuckle sounded musical. "And I know you'll just keep asking them until someone answers."

When Frankie turned to leave the office, she saw the back wall for the first time. The sliding door took up half the wall space. On the other half hung one large photograph. A very familiar image.

A girl, eight or nine, no one was sure. Standing in front of a picture window of an orbital space station. Fingertips on the window. Eyes wide open, mouth pressed tightly closed. Tracks of tears from her eyes to her chin. A drop on the edge of her chin. The camera had focused tight on her, blocking out the panic and horror of the dozens of people behind her.

The camera showed a slice of the world outside, but it failed to show what the girl could never stop staring at. Her planet—her world—collapsing in on itself, after the deadliest so-called munitions mistake in Cooperative Realm history.

The photographer who flash-messaged the photo to her news boss had called it "Child Orphan of Wala."

So Frankie would remain, forever. The photo ran with every first-day story. Every opinion piece. Every time one of the many legal actions came up. Every stupid anniversary of the annihilation of her people.

Frankie couldn't help straightening her posture, self-consciously tugging at her unruly hair, smoothing her dress. She hadn't actually looked at the picture in years. Much as she'd wished it, not much had changed. She still pushed her hair back the same way, and it fell forward anyway. She still cried in silence, alone. Trying not to be a burden.

"A striking photograph. So obviously true."

Monica Valdes had come up behind her. "I idolized that girl. So strong. To be dragged to the capital city. To stand up for yourselves, when the regent wanted you to keep on parading around on that 'apology tour.'

"It was all I could do to get up every day, trying to avoid the worst of the violence in my family, and here you six girls were, standing so solemn in front of giant assemblies, forced to accept apologies from adults with bitter agendas with tact and grace."

"My brother knew I treasured the picture. He had it printed on a handkerchief, so he could stand in front of me and blow his nose on it." Valdes took in a quick breath, as if she were holding back tears. "I stole it, and took it with me when I ran."

Frankie turned to look at Valdes. Her violet eyes shimmered, her lip twitched. She shook her head the slightest bit, and stiffened her shoulders, regaining control.

"Now, I help other girls die, so to speak. They give up everything—status, power, a comfortable life. I don't know how they hear about me. The girls we help are told never to contact home or friends again. But more girls keep calling me; I have a dead-drop messaging service." She shrugged. "I have to help."

She frowned at Frankie. "I would never have believed that you would turn into one of these weekend people, people with so much money and so little empathy they think nothing of watching a person in pain. I admit, it threw me for a loop."

Frankie thought she'd felt raw before. Now she was flayed and turned over an open flame.

"I'm sorry," she said. What a pathetic thing to say.

"Can I give you a hug?" Monica Valdes said.

As they left Valdes's offices, Frankie's mind swirled and eddied, playing over all she'd seen. All she'd learned.

Relief washed through her.

Nobody was dying. Nobody was even being hurt.

Well, if you didn't count the monster humans who Monica Valdes was duping into paying for the opportunity to watch her lie to them. And use their credits to save the girls they probably wouldn't even notice in their daily lives.

The quiet resort now felt like a place of solace as she made her way through the softly lit passages.

Spike's tail had stopped its angry swishing, too.

She thought of Aimee, and of the other brave, desperate young women who risked everything to set themselves free. Sure, Frankie was a "child orphan," but she hadn't chosen anything. Things had just happened to her. In the same situation, would she have been as brave?

As they passed through the main dome of the tech village, Frankie's footsteps echoed on the textured floor, a steady rhythm that grounded her. The smells of solvents and oils had diminished, letting the lightest taste of the ocean come through. The sounds of sleeping machines gave a background hum to the sleeping resort.

And the sharks! Who would have guessed they'd turn out to be allies. Beings both monstrous and clever. No wonder Dr. Mazur was so delighted to put up with the endless rush of tourists in order to work here. She had a whole new society to learn about. Its own ways and traditions, hidden deep beneath the surface.

When she reached the passageway leading to the VIP area, Frankie stepped into the lounge. The softly pulsing lights along the window supports gently guided them home.

They strode straight through the now-empty lounge, and into the passage to the guest rooms. For a moment, Frankie thought of detouring into the dining room and onto the kitchen, to see if she could scare up something to eat.

Too much work.

Bed was calling.

Was it wrong to let people believe they had witnessed a death? Why appeal to their base desires? On the other hand, nobody forced them to come here. Spend their credit.

Caveat emptor, asswipes.

Her steps grew heavier and heavier. The engine was dry. All she could think of was sleep. Delicious sleep

As she keyed in the code for her guest room's door, Frankie yawned wide. Spike yawned even wider.

As they entered the guest room, Spike bounded ahead, her claws clicking on the floor. She leaped onto the bed, circling a spot at the foot before settling down with a contented burp.

"Fine,"Frankie said, kicking her sandals into the walk-in closet next to the still-open door. "You can share the bed. But leave me a pillow this time, okay?"

Spike's ears twitched, and she tilted her head, gauging Frankie's level of seriousness. Frankie tried to look as serious as possible, but her eyes were drooping. Spike pawed at two pillows, but pulled only one closer to her chosen spot.

As the door shut, Frankie didn't bother waving the room lights on. Walking toward the bed, she tried shrug out of her bolero jacket, which, as it turned out, wasn't the warmest jacket in the world.

Suddenly, a low, menacing hiss cut through the room. Frankie's head snapped up, her eyes immediately seeking out Spike.

The cyvlossic was crouched at the foot of the bed, her fur bristling and her muscles coiled tight. Her intense gaze was fixed on the window, her body poised as if ready to launch herself at it.

Frankie turned to look.

A stranger in diving gear was treading water was right outside.

153

Chapter Twenty-One

Frankie's fatigue vanished under a whoosh of adrenaline as she stared at the bulked-up diver treading water directly outside her window.

Her mouth went dry. A cold sweat broke out on her skin. Without the bolero jacket, her arms were bare. Exposed.

Spike's low, menacing growl filled the room. Her fur bristling and muscles coiled tight, she launched off the bed and onto the recliner closest to the window, ready to fling herself at the intruder. Like that was even possible, Frankie thought wildly. There was no airlock in this room.

Was there?

Then Spike relaxed.

The cyvlossic's growl eased, shifted tone, forming a single word.

"Gem."

"Gum?" Frankie said, not daring to moving her gaze from the swimmer. Then she understood.

Gem Strand, Shepherd Station's head of security. And, apparently leader of the SystA dive recovery team.

And not exactly a fan of hers.

Emotions cascaded over Frankie. Relief at the familiar face—well the cranky green eyes behind the half-mask, at least. Irritation. A growing sense of unease. She hadn't called for help.

Why was Gem here now?

And why did they feel the need to make such a freakishly dramatic entrance?

Gem lifted a wrist, pantomiming the opening of a communications app. Frankie fumbled for her own wristcom, which she'd left on the bed back when dinner was going to be a celebration. Her fingers fumbled at the range sensor and the encryption codes until she heard a burst of annoyed breathing.

"Sansom. Where is she?" Gem's voice crackled through the device, sticky with displeasure. "As soon as we got scrambled and down here, her tracker went dead. It's in your shower, I think. Got her tied up in there?"

The joke fell flat, laced as it was with an undercurrent of anger.

Frankie bristled at the accusation, her own temper rising to meet Gem's. She shook her head vehemently, her words coming out in a sharp, clipped tone. "No rescue. We don't need you. We didn't call."

Gem's eyes narrowed. They swatted a curious anglerfish away.

"Not your call."

"We're all fine here."

"You don't get to decide that. Call Bruce. Use the emergency number. You do like those."

Ugh. Annoyance flared in her chest—trust Gem to show up unannounced and start barking orders.

Frankie's fingers flew across the wristcom.

Five beeps, six. Frustration built a new home in her chest with each unanswered beep. Bruce's silence was deafening, and a sinking feeling settled in her gut. Why wasn't he picking up? Wasn't this exactly the kind of situation where she needed his guidance, his support?

She shrugged her shoulders. Another fail.

"We're not blowing this mission because of you," Gem snapped, their voice cutting through Frankie's spiraling thoughts. "I'm coming in. Meet me at the pool." They tapped the side of their mask, probably the comms system since the call went dead, and dropped out of sight.

Frankie stared at the empty space where Gem had been. She felt like she'd been slapped, Gem's words ringing in her ears. Failing? Is that what Gem thought of her? After everything she'd done, all the risks she'd taken?

Were they wrong?

Spike butted her head against Frankie's leg, urging her to move. Frankie looked down at her companion, seeing the urgency in Spike's eyes.

"Why didn't you back me up?" She took a deep breath, trying to center herself, to push down the rising tide of panic and frustration.

Everything was slipping out of her control. Again.

They raced through the resort's empty passageways. Still quiet, still empty, still blue, but the lights seemed to be moving faster.

At the pool's airlock, Frankie made sure to close both doors.

She had to step carefully through the locker area. A servo had apparently just washed the floor, leaving it wet and smelling like a pine forest. The mostly empty dome, with the air tank fillers off and the people gone, echoed with the gentle lapping of water against the pool's edges.

The muted underwater lighting cast a shimmering, ethereal

glow across the surface of the pool, transforming it into a mesmer-izing kaleidoscope of blues and greens.

Gem was already waiting, perched on the edge of the pool with their flippers off, feet on the shelf under the water. Their air tanks were still strapped to their back, and it didn't look like they were taking them off.

The rough texture at the pool's edge bit into Frankie's bare feet as she approached, a stark contrast to the plush carpeting of the resort's corridors.

Spike loped over to the far side of the pool. Frankie was too tired to follow right away.

Gem eyed Frankie critically.

"You look terrible, by the way," Gem said, their tone dry, their voice high with helium. "But the dress looks good on you."

Frankie ignored the jab. "You can't be here! This place is all over surveillance." Her voice came out a screeching whisper

Gem rolled their eyes."Like we didn't bring signal blockers."

"Blockers only buy you a little time."

"The plan, thanks for asking, is to grab the girl, toss her into one of the emergency submersibles, and blow it. It'll take her eight hours to get out of it, but at least she'll be alive."

"You can't!" Frankie cried, her voice a hideous squeak. "There's already a plan!"

"What plan?" Gem squeaked, looking mad. "That is the plan."

Frankie shook her head, tears of frustration stung the corners of her eyes. She took a deep breath, the pine-tinged air burning her lungs.

"Listen—" she started.

The airlock hatch crashed open. The sound ricocheted off the dome's ceiling like a gunshot.

Monica Valdes glided in, her presence commanding and chilling, even in a flannel shirt and yoga pants. In her hand, she held a Sturbridge laser gun. She held it like she knew how to use it.

Gem was on their feet.

Frankie was still on the side of the pool closest to the door. Valdes reached her first.

"You invited a guest?" she asked Frankie, her voice deceptively soft.

Samir Russo arrived a heartbeat later, lungs blown and legs unsteady. He slid on the wet flooring, but recovered enough not to fall.

Valdes leveled the gun at Gem, eyes cold, hand firm. "Russo. Take the air tank."

Gem's hand flew to their belt, whipping out a weapon of her own. The two stood locked in a tense standoff.

"Um," Russo said. "Okay if I come over?"

Frankie leaped at Valdes, blocking her ability to target Gem. Spike reared up on her hind legs, startling Gem and buying them a precious second.

"Everybody just calm down," Frankie squeaked out. "We're on the same side."

She turned to Gem, her words tumbling out in a rush as she explained the truth behind the resort's activities—the witness protection program, the staged deaths, the unlikely alliance with the monstrush sharks.

The sharks drew a thoughtful "huh" from Gem.

As Frankie spoke, the tension in the room slowly ebbed, the gentle lapping of the pool's water a soothing counterpoint to the gravity of her words. The pine scent, thankfully, was fading.

Gem's eyes widened, a mix of disbelief and grudging respect.

"Seriously? That's a ridiculously complicated plan. Sounds like something we'd do." Their tone held a note of approval.

They lowered their weapon slowly, as did Valdes. The tension in the room eased but did not ebb.

"I understand," Gem said. "We stepped on another operation. We'll back off."

"Good," said Valdes.

Nobody moved.

"Right," Gem said, their gaze flicking between Frankie and Valdes. "Guess we'll head out then. The girl's life is still on you, though, Crowe."

Gem had remembered Frankie's cover identity.

"The girl's life is on me," Valdes said. "Get out."

"Nice to see you again, too, Monica." Gem grinned and sat down to put their flippers on. "Gotta get up to the station sometime. People will forget you're alive."

Frankie looked at Gem, and then Valdes. Spike snorted.

Of course they knew each other.

"Do I look like I belong in vacuum."

"Couldn't hurt to ask," Gem said, looking at the mask straps they were fiddling with and not at Monica Valdes. "Crowe," she said, settling the mask on their face. "You still owe us, though. Eight hours in a bends-tank is at least four beers each."

Gem settled the mouthpiece in place and gracefully took to the water. They waved once as they sank down, then blasted out of sight of the pool in a flurry of flippers.

Frankie watched them go, a mix of relief and exhaustion washing over her.

"Sorry," she said. "We got our signals crossed."

"Always an adventure with Gem," Valdes agreed. "Surprised you put up with them." She checked her comm. "It's almost tomorrow already. How about we call it a night?"

If only they could.

Chapter Twenty-Two

F rankie collapsed backwards onto the bed, the soft whir of
its antigrav mechanism working overtime to tone the
sway down.

Finally.

No young women to save. No insinuations, no threats. No
guns! No stranger divers at the window. Nothing out there now
but gray-black water and some glowy stringy things moving slow.

Her dress, once so elegant, now had water stains on the hem
from the pool. She wriggled out of it, letting it fall to the floor in a
silken heap.

She should get up and get ready for bed, but here she was
already in bed. And so, so ready for sleep.

Based on her observations of Spike's many naps, the bed would
wait two minutes before wrapping its warm self around her like a
cocoon. Despite the slight coolness of the air against her skin,
Frankie decided to wait it out rather than figure out anything
complicated like how blankets work.

This day had gone on way too long. Was it only this morning

that she thought that this was a simple case of a dive instructor gone bad? Would one of these assignments ever turn out to be so easy?

Her breathing started to slow. Spike was snoring softly somewhere. The lounger? The foot of the bed? She'd think about it later.

The soft embrace of the bed startled her awake.

And then she couldn't sleep.

Seriously?

Now every time Frankie closed her eyes, images of the night's events played out like grainy videos inside her mind. Aimee's fury, Valdes and her many offices, Gem out of nowhere, the total weirdness of smelling a pine forest while standing two hundred meters under the sea.

With a groan, Frankie hauled herself out of bed and stumbled over to bathroom. In the light of a jellyfish-shaped nightlight, she grabbed the carafe of water and took a long swig out of it. Too bad she didn't have a sugary drink packet to pour in there. Evelyn Crowe, heir to a soft drink empire, surely would have.

At least she didn't have to pretend to be Evelyn Crowe any more.

She dragged her feet on the grassy carpet, tingly cool at this hour. Time for the full Frankie relaxation outfit: soft-soft pajama bottoms plus gnarly Angry Vibes t-shirt from their fourth-to-the-last concert tour. Or was it fifth, now?

Still carrying the carafe, she picked up the plush bath robe she hadn't hung up this morning. She draped herself along the lounger closest to the window and then draped the robe over herself.

Up close, now she could see there was more out there than those glowy string thingies. There were the round dark thingies, and floating yellow fan-plants. Dr. Mazur would be so disappointed that Frankie had already forgotten all their proper names.

She was lucky she could even remember her own name at the moment.

Any of them.

Frankie could've sworn she had not fallen asleep when a jarring bang jolted her awake.

Her room swayed. Then a long hiss.

Hull breach.

Spike, curled up at the foot of the bed, leapt to her feet, fur bristling and ears pinned back.

The sound seemed to have come from the passageway, right next door.

They had to get out of here. Frankie pulled the robe on, and grabbed Spike around the middle.

And immediately dropped Spike on the floor. The cyvlossic was faster than her, already at the door and pushing on the cabinet panel beside it. The cabinet cover popped off, spilling emergency breathers and an air tent on the ground.

Frankie scooped them up with one hand and touched the door with the other.

Not hot, good. Wait, that was a different kind of emergency. She put her ear to the door. It didn't sound like water was rushing past.

She pressed the panel to open the door. As it descended into the floor, she could see the passageway was clear.

Jamming the emergency supplies into the big pockets of her robe, she stepped out.

A yellow light was spinning at the end of the hall, a miniature version of the light that spun at the top of the emergency station near the labyrinth outside. Frankie crept toward the light.

She peered out of the porthole beneath the light, and saw the ocean beyond.

She should have been seeing inside the emergency submersible.

The spherical vehicle, designed to transport distressed guests safely to the surface, was gone.

Footsteps echoed down the passageway.

Frankie turned to see Monica Valdes loping towards her. The resort owner was still dressed in the same burnt-orange wrap dress from earlier, her silver hair slightly mussed. Close behind her came Sylvana Patel, fully dressed and alert, followed by a yawning Samir Russo in black baggy trousers. The two bigger dining room staffers, each in a complete sweatsuit set, brought up the rear.

"What happened?" Valdes demanded.

"I don't know," Frankie squeaked.

Everyone winced.

Frankie swallowed hard, and tried to pitch her voice lower. "I heard a giant rumble, and when I came out, the submersible was gone."

Patel stepped forward, examining the now-empty space. "Not an accident. Someone used the controls and jettisoned the sub."

Valdes turned to Frankie, her gaze sharp. "What do you know about this? Did you have anything to do with this?"

Frankie blinked, taken aback by the accusation. Her frazzled mind flashed to Gem's garbled comment about using a submersible. Was that something? She shook her head.

"No, of course not. I was asleep until the noise woke me up."

Valdes held her gaze for a moment longer, then nodded, apparently satisfied. Patel, meanwhile, had sprinted back down the passageway, her footsteps fading into the distance.

An uncomfortable silence settled over the group, broken only by the soft pulse of the strobing yellow light.

Patel returned, slightly out of breath. "Nathan Henderson," she said, scowling. "He's not in his room."

Valdes pulled up a floating screen interface. A grid of views from multiple cameras flashed past.

"There he is. Took two big bags in with him." She glanced at Patel. "He knew the code? The alarm didn't sound."

Patel shrugged. "He's a long-timer. Of course I gave him the code."

Valdes sighed, rubbing at her temple. Even now, just out of bed, her hair was perfect. She turned to Russo and the two dining hall servers. "Thank you for your help. You can go back to bed now."

The two servers nodded and trudged back down the passageway, their footsteps heavy with fatigue. Russo stayed, looking out the now scenic emergency door.

"Henderson." Valdes groaned, watching them. "Why now?"

A nagging sense of guilt tugged at Frankie. Or rather, a nagging tug on the bathrobe by Spike.

"Um," she said, her voice small in the passageway. "Well, I overheard Henderson and Watike arguing. About you."

Valdes's head snapped up, her eyes narrowing. "You've got to be kidding," she said, her tone a mix of exasperation and resignation. "Now he catches a clue?"

Frankie shifted uncomfortably. "He said he didn't have a car reserved. He wanted me to leave early with him. I said I'd take him, but not until tomorrow. Today," she corrected, glancing at her wristcom.

Russo looked up from inspecting the latch mechanism at the foot of the airlock door, his brow furrowing. "Why didn't he wait, then?"

Valdes sighed, her shoulders slumping. "You know him. Not a shred of patience. If he has to go, it must be right now. Or never."

Frankie squinted, trying to remember the conversation through the haze of fatigue. "I think he actually used those words. 'Now or never.'"

Valdes and Patel exchanged a long look, some unspoken communication passing between them. Finally, Valdes nodded.

"We'll need to move another submersible to this corridor," she said, her tone businesslike. "We can't leave our guests without an emergency exit."

Patel nodded. "I can disengage one near the family village. They have two extra. Russo, help me move it over?"

Russo gave a mock salute. "Me and my trusty float pallet are ready to serve. Ten minutes?"

"Fifteen."

Valdes and Patel started down the passageway, their heads bent together as they discussed the logistics of retrieving Henderson's submersible and the potential fallout from his impulsive actions. Their voices faded into the distance, leaving Frankie and Russo alone in the empty corridor.

Russo leaned against the wall, his easy smile a balm. "Did you get any sleep at all?" he asked, his voice soft.

"Not much. You?"

"Nah. Too much gnarly action."

They stood in silence for a moment, watching a family of glowing fish sail over the passageway. This world was so different from her own. Not land. Not space. Something different. Something beautiful.

Too bad she didn't have time for another dive. The only dive left on the schedule was the killer one, at mid-morning. And she was definitely not doing that one. No matter the shark attack wasn't "real," Frankie didn't want to be any part of it.

"You know," Russo said, pushing himself off the wall, "if you're not gonna sleep anyways, might as well come with me."

"Outside? Now?" Suddenly, Frankie was wide awake.

"Now's prime for critter watching. The sun's coming up. It'll hit us in about twenty minutes. You can catch the night guys heading to bed and the day guys just starting to stir."

Russo grinned, a puppy ready to play. "It's such a bummer on these weekends, nobody ever wants to do the sunrise dive. Everybody wants to dive the boring mid-morning one." A shadow of something—pain?—flitted across his face, but cleared almost before Frankie could be sure that she'd seen it. "But here you are, and here I am."

Frankie hesitated, glancing back at her room. Spike had already retreated inside, no doubt curled up on the bed again. The thought of trying to sleep now, with her mind buzzing and her body thrumming with adrenaline, seemed impossible.

Compared to another chance to see this wild world outside.

"Sure," she said. "Why not?"

Chapter Twenty-Three

Samir Russo kept a stash of protein bars in the diving room dome. And healthy green juice drinks.

Thank Safra.

"Is this one of yours?" he asked Frankie as she sucked hers down. She felt as if she hadn't eaten in weeks. "I mean, one of your family's drinks?" he clarified.

Frankie stopped slurping to blink at him, confused. Then she remembered: Evelyn Crowe was the heir to a healthy-drinks empire.

"Do you like it?" she said.

"Best brand going," he said smacking his lips. "Drinking one makes you want to drink another one right away."

Frankie was about to say, yes, it was one of hers, when he went on.

"If you do drink two in a row, though, your poo turns blue. Which is weird, you know? Because the drink is green."

Frankie bit her tongue.

The diving pool dome was just as dark as before, but somehow much less scary when you were smiling. The pine scent had faded, exposing the brine and oil of diving gear.

He checked her gear and she checked his. They were using the sticky-face comms again.

"Jin told me about your suit, how it was faked up," Russo said, checking her straps. "Sorry about that. Not everybody in the biz is legit."

"No worries," she said. "I didn't pay that much for them, anyway. And I like the big wide helmet."

"Mask," Russo corrected. "Spacer." He winked.

He stepped into the pool, dropping into the water and immediately pivoting toward the open water beyond. Frankie followed a moment later.

Out in the water, among the ocean's night crowd, Frankie could see how the resort complemented its surroundings. Much like the see-through jellyfish, the transparent tunnels and domes that connected the various sections of the complex were like veins and organs of a living, breathing entity, sharing its life and energy with the sea.

The family village was at the opposite end of the resort from the VIP area. It was actually a shorter path to swim to it than to walk. Above them, the water began to gradually lighten, the sun ray's slowly stretching down.

The stretch of sandy park ahead of the family village was dominated by the Coral Carousel. A breathtaking rainbow of vibrant coral species adorned the towering spiral structure.

Delicate branches of staghorn coral swayed in the gentle current, their intricate forms like a tiny, vertical forest. Nearby, the ruffled edges of fiery red coral pulsed with a soft, glow, each undulation drawing little silverfish in and out.

Frankie wasn't going anywhere near the coral.

The comm system crackled.

"Like a cosmic dance, isn't it?" Russo said. "The way every-thing moves and flows together. Only thing, watch out for sea snakes."

"They won't bite?"

"Nope. Harmless to humans, unless you're a pretty lady with a scary story from the past. Aimee told me about her freakout yester-day. You saved the day."

Frankie waved off the compliment. "I had help." She'd needed it.

A school of translucent, ribbon-like creatures undulated past, their slender bodies shimmering yellow and red.

"What are they?" she asked, her voice hushed with awe.

"Some kind of ctenophore, I think," Samir replied. "Like cosmic jellies, riding the stellar winds of the sea."

Frankie didn't see any sea snakes. But as they continued past the carousel, she felt a tickle on her arm and looked down to see a tiny, electric-blue nudibranch crawling across her suit. Its feathery gills and neon coloring were like nothing she had ever seen. Russo gently coaxed the creature onto his hand and set it on a path back to the coral, his movements fluid and purposeful.

Frankie followed Russo to the spare submersible. It hung free, attached to the dome only at the middle by a thick rope. Chief Patel must have already detached it.

Russo expertly pulled the knot out and tied it further down the center of the sphere, making a sort of rein. He clipped a tiny device at the apex of the rein, where his hand would have been.

"Check this out," he said.

The device hummed to life. It expanded into a narrow tube, perpendicular to the sphere. Russo let go of it and looked at the buttons on his wristcom.

Frankie realized she was still wearing her wristcom.

Her vacuum-standard one. It wasn't rated for water pressure.

So much for that.

Russo looked up. The sphere started to move on its own. No, the little stick was pulling it. A stick not one-hundredth the mass of that sphere.

"Bleeding cool." Russo said. "Watike's design. Prototype, but just wait. It's gonna be a game changer."

In the distance, a pair of curious rosicants played among the swaying fronds of a tall, flopsy kelp forest. The spotted patterns along the sleek fur on their sides served as camouflage in the dappled daytime light among the kelp. This early, though, the spots stood out.

"Wait," Frankie said. "How did those guys get in here?" Both rosicants were as wide as she was, and a good bit longer. The security barrier should have kept them out.

"Hey, the rosies are here!" Russo said. "Lucky day, us. Swim closer, slowly, and see if they'll play. I'll park this big ball on idle for a minute, and be right with you.

Closer, she could see that what she thought were shades of gray fur were actually a mottled blend of deep blues and greens. The slightly larger one, noticed her. It glided out of the forest and toward her, its powerful flukes propelling it like a rocket.

As it approached, it chirruped, a series of high-pitched clicks and whistles.

Frankie felt a gentle tug on her arm, and turned to see Russo smiling at her, his eyes crinkling. "She's saying hello," he said. "rosicants are super friendly."

The animal drew closer, its companion following a little more slowly. Now Frankie could see the intricate patterns of their fur, each spot and squiggle unique.

The leader, now a long arm's length away, slowed its approach and regarded Frankie with a tilted head, its black eyes bright and inquisitive.

Russo slowly extended his hand, palm up, towards the creature. "Let it come to you," he whispered. "They're very gentle, but they can be a bit shy at first."

Frankie mimicked his motion, holding her breath. She didn't want to scare the rosie. She wanted to hug it.

The rosicant hesitated for a moment, then slowly stretched out its long snout, nuzzling Russo's gloved hand. Its handful of whiskers, long and delicate, brushed against his fingers.

Emboldened by its partner's actions, the second rosicant approached Frankie, its movements graceful and so, so careful. It came in a one-quarter speed, compared with its friend. That one now had flipped upside down. Russo slowly stroked its underbelly.

"See the flap, here?" he said, pointing to a crease between the side fin and the mammal's body. "We put a little chip in there. When we find friendly rosies, we chip 'em. That way, they can go in and out of the safety fence. And we can say hi."

Something gently bumped Frankie's outstretched hand. She gasped, but didn't stop the slow treading that was keeping her in place.

The sensation of the rosicant's fur against her skin made her shiver with pleasure. The silky smooth strands together merged into a texture like illustrated velvet.

As she ran her fingers down its side, the rosicant let out a soft, trilling purr, a sound that seemed to vibrate through Frankie's entire body.

She needed to touch it, mammal to mammal. Skin to skin.

"Can I take my glove off?" she said.

"Sorry, no." Russo said. "We humans carry bad germs, sometimes. Who knows where your hand's been lately? No offense."

No worries. The creature's scent, carried an upsweeping current, was a surprising mix of brine and something sweet, like ripe fruit.

Soon, the creatures had had enough. They disengaged, darting around the divers in a whirlwind of bubbles and tiny bits of green.

They chased each other back to the kelp forest, their clicks and whistles filling the water with a joyful symphony.

Frankie found herself laughing, the weight of the past few days momentarily lifted from her shoulders. The rosicants looped and spun, their movements an aquatic ballet. Were they putting on a show for their new friends?

The sunlight had reached them now. It was getting harder and harder to keep track of the rosicants. They chased each other deeper and deeper into the forest, and through the safety barrier.

Then they were gone.

It was a moment of pure enchantment, a memory that would stay with her forever. A reminder that wonders exist in the depths of the ocean as well as the universe.

Chapter Twenty-Four

Frankie almost didn't get up in time for the big event.

Wiped out by—well, every single blessed thing this whole entire weekend—she'd dropped into her bed after the dive, lost to the world.

Spike had to escalate from the usual persistent kneading to outright yowling at her blanket-covered head to even get a reaction.

"I heard you," Frankie groaned. "Go on without me."

"On the clock."

No way Bruce would dock her for not watching the not-killing. Right?

"Just go, already."

"Coward."

"Am not." She flung the covers off her face to glare at Spike.

Who winked.

Ugh. Spike could really push her buttons. Who ever thought it was a good idea to give a cyvlossic a voice box, anyway?

"Fine."

By the time she was dressed and they got to the viewing lounge, the other swimmers had come in from the dive.

The furniture in the space had been rearranged. The shorter benches—loveseats—had been moved to form a single line in front of the window overlooking the abyss. They hadn't been dragged—the beautiful grass floor looked pristine.

The resort's other guests, a handful still damp from the dive, perched in various states of anticipation on the plush, too-forgiving seats.

Ready to view some carnage.

Outside, she could see only Aimee and Russo. One small and frail, in the twilight world of this ocean; the other bulkier, solid, more at home.

Aimee, in a sky blue short diving suit, was piggybacking air from Russo's tanks, just like in the videos. Russo seemed to be pointing out something near the fence—a little fish? He gestured that they should travel along the fence to follow it.

On the viewing benches, some of the couples clasped hands tightly. Others sat apart from their partner. All held tension palpable in their postures. Against the happy burble of the wonder-water ambient music, their squeaky side conversations cut through. The small gray lady sat near the middle, spine erect, face steady on the divers outside, following every kick and glide.

CapCity vultures. Frankie could almost taste their morbid curiosity, the tantalizing allure of witnessing something forbidden. Something raw. Something they thought was real.

Happy Elysium Weekend!

Monica Valdes stood a few meters behind the spectators, her arms crossed as she leaned against the wall that separated the dining room from the rest of the space. She watched the scene with an expression that read from a distance as detachment. But her hands were fists.

The floating orb-lights around her—around the whole room—were all dimmed, to not distract from the view outside.

Frankie skirted the viewing area, and approached Valdes. The resort owner was back in silver today, a sort of pantsuit, the legs flaring wide toward the ankles like a tail.

Spike did not follow her. The cyvlossic padded to the only empty loveseat, by the far wall. The seat obviously waiting for them, the last guests. Spike perched on the cushion with enough space left for Frankie to join her.

Yeah, right.

"Just in time," Valdes said softly.

Someone was missing, though.

"How's Henderson? Heard anything?" The eight hours was surely up by now.

Valdes scoffed, more than a hint of irritation flashing across her face.

"We picked him up, of course. I had to ask my assistant to cut her vacation short to go fetch the submersible. And Nathan, of course." She shook her head. "Good riddance."

The air still carried that subtle blend of moonflower and spices, but nothing felt soothing today.

Outside, the swimmers had reached the right point in the security fence. Closest to the abyss.

Valdes pushed off the wall. She stood straight and still. Arms crossed, she held each elbow in her hand so tightly she was in danger of breaking it. Frankie stood close to her, as if to catch her if she fell.

Russo made a series of gestures, guiding Aimee ever closer to the edge.

Everyone on the benches leaned forward. Intent on the action.

Frankie's breath caught in her throat, memories of those grainy video recordings flashing through her mind. The girl in the pink bikini, the blood blooming in the water, the monster shark rising from the depths...

She forced herself to swallow, push down the growing sense of dread.

Now, primed by all she'd learned, Frankie saw the scene differently. She picked upon the subtle cues, the carefully choreographed dance between Aimee and Russo.

When Russo appeared to slice across Aimee's midriff, Frankie caught the shadow of something in Aimee's hand, the source of the crimson cloud that started to billow around her.

At the window, gasps and murmurs rippled through the gathered guests. Some leaned so far toward the window they were in danger of tipping out of their seats, while others recoiled. The tiny gray lady did not react, but continued to watch, avid.

So satisfied.

Frankie went cold.

Russo pushed Aimee past the boundary. Aimee clutched her abdomen and thrashed convincingly.

The monstrush mother shark rose from the abyss, its massive form casting a shadow over the scene.

A collective gasp tore through the room. Frankie's heart stuttered, even though she knew the truth.

Aimee's body went suddenly stiff in a convincing display of terror.

The shark's jaws closed around Aimee's body, pushing the woman and the top half of the shark down, obscuring them from view. Couples clutched at each other, some turning away, unable to watch. Others leaped up, racing to the window, trying to see past the edge of the abyss.

But Frankie kept her eyes on the shark's flukes, marveling at the precision of the dive. The intricacy of the deception.

The shark's movements were too calculated to be the frenzy of a mindless predator. It was a dance, a carefully orchestrated performance that left the audience breathless and believing in the lie.

A new blood trail followed the shark's head as it gently floated up and into view. Parts of the fake-Aimee decoy hung from her mouth. A quite realistic looking foot and leg, except the skin wasn't exactly right.

A torn bit of sky-blue suit hung out of the corner of her mouth, apparently stuck between teeth. Russo probably got the suit bits from the "danger box" they'd found in the pool dome.

The shark shook the fake-Aimee-meat back and forth a few times, as if the rest of Aimee had jammed in her gullet and needed to be loosened before she could be completely swallowed down.

Then all the meat was gone.

Still hungry—always hungry—the shark turned her head this way and that, trying to sense more prey.

For a moment, the shark turned its gaze directly at the observation window.

Everyone in the front seats froze. Even Spike, whose ears flicked back hard.

Chef's kiss. Icing on the cake. A masterful final bit of performance.

The shark pretended to see something below her. In a flash, she was gone.

All she'd left behind was a little blood emptying itself in the wide water and an audience full of stupefied humans.

Frankie saw shock, horror, and a perverse sense of euphoria mingled on their faces. They would leave this place believing they had been privy to something deeply taboo, never knowing the truth behind the illusion.

For a good few minutes, the guests sat or stood still, processing what they believed they had witnessed.

Except for one.

The tiny gray lady was on her feet and beelining toward Valdes before the fake-Aimee blood had fully dispersed.

"Miss Valdes," she started. Her voice had that weird vibrato in the center. "This is untenable." She waved toward the window. "I've attended this event—this weekend—twice now."

Twice? Once wasn't enough?

Frankie's feelings must have shown on her face. Valdes gave her a warning glance and then looked down as the smaller woman turned back to her.

"Your honor?"

"And both times, the moment—the exact moment—is hidden from us."

"You mean when the shark dipped below the ledge for a second?"

"A full second!" The gray lady seemed to puff up, seething. "And there's nothing left to see!"

Monica Valdes said nothing for a second. A second second. A third.

"I understand," she said, the consummate hospitality profes-sional. "I'll speak to the shark."

The gray lady huffed, not sure how to react. She knew one didn't just speak to sharks. Her demand was impossible to fulfill.

As the guests began to disperse, their voices hushed and their steps unsteady—she refused to call it giddy—Frankie ambled toward Spike. She dropped on the loveseat in the space the cyvlossic had left for her. They bumped shoulders.

"Scum," Spike said, looking at the empty benches.

"Asswipes," Frankie said.

"Shark turds."

"You win. Let's go home."

Chapter Twenty-Five

As the air limo purred along the double-wide transit tube, away from Valdes Underwater Resort, Frankie finally started to unwind. Half an hour into the eight-hour return trip to the surface, she let the cool embrace of the plush seat draw her into calm. She let the autovalet hand her a ula berry juice.

They better be right about this depressurizing-timing thing. She didn't want to end this weekend with a bad case of the bends.

She sighed, trying again to let the worries go. She sipped the tangy juice, swallowed hard to make her ears pop. That was a worry for later. Seven whole hours later.

Brilliant idea to make the top of this transit tube clear. It felt like an extension of the resort. On the trip in, the view led you down into wonder, teasing what was to come. On the trip out, it let you hang on to the wonder just a a tiny bit longer as you transitioned back to the outer world.

Frankie gazed out, hoping to see that pair of playful rosicants. Rosies! No sign of them, but plenty of those fat blue jellies and darting silver schools of fish. The water was growing brighter; already they were out of the twilight depth.

Beside her, Spike shifted restlessly, the cyvlossic's discomfort palpable. Going back up, even as slowly as the limo was taking them, seemed to be as hard on Spike as the descent had been. Frankie reached out, running her fingers through Spike's tufted gray and black fur, feeling the warmth emanating from her companion's body. "Just a little longer," she murmured, her voice soft and reassuring. "We'll be back on solid ground soon."

Spike's dulled eyes met hers, a flicker of understanding passing between them. The cyvlossic's ears twitched.

"Next hotel, I pick," she groan/growled.

Frankie couldn't stop her chuckle. Picturing Spike, the queen of don't-bother-me, dealing with the many maddening details to plan their next getaway was both amusing and endearing.

"Don't tell me," she said, resting her hand on Spike's shoulders. "Tell Bruce."

At the second turnoff, a little half-domed cul-de-sac where they'd spend the next forty minutes waiting out the pressure, Frankie stepped out of the car. Walking toward the dome's edge, scaring off a turtle-thing, she tried, again, to call Bruce.

No answer, but at least the signal went through. She'd try again at the next turnoff.

She'd finished her mission report already, in a final burst of energy while waiting for her car to be ready. If Bruce would just pick up his messages, they could wrap up this assignment and be done done done.

She could see the top of the coral carousel, its spiral fading into a wavy point at the top. She'd thought the coral would be the highlight—just the idea that thousands of tiny, fragile, apparently non-sentient creatures would join up to form giant, sturdy structures made her head spin.

But it was the rosies she would remember, and not only because of the cute nickname. Their fur! The spark of play—and speculation—in their eyes. Frankie wanted to bring one home. Two.

What if she used half of her ship's giant cargo hold to make a giant water tank? It would have to be a box, so she could change the pressure and salinity. And, you know, keep the water in.

After her trip to the beach a while back, she'd had the same thought. How hard could it be?

Crazy hard.

But maybe worth it?

Nobody she knew was hauling live water animals. She could create a niche for herself. Was there a market for such a service? She could create one.

Yeah, right.

Or she could just lie back here, grab another ula juice, and continue to pick up missions from Bruce. Supposing they ever got a hold of him again.

At the next turnoff, Frankie persuaded Spike to get out of the car.

"You know, Monica said walking would dislodge the bubbles," she said coaxingly. "Make it better."

Spike growled something cranky that Frankie let just roll on over her. The cyvlossic lurched off the seat and onto the rubbery flooring of the half dome.

Frankie left her. She stepped closer to the window. On this level a few hardy plants had latched onto the shelf at the edge of the window where it met the floor of the dome. Their yellow-and-green striped tendrils attracted those bubble-shaped fish, the ones with the spiky spines, not the ones with the puffy cheeks. She'd already forgotten their names.

Dr. Mazur would shake her head in disappointment. Or, more

likely, resignation. How many weekend tourists had she talked to over the months? Describing the sea world she knew so well to people whose memories would never hold a bit of it. Frankie didn't envy her that job.

She tried Bruce again.

No answer.

The vibrant colors of the fish and the graceful sway of the underwater plants painted a picture of serenity. A happy deception. This world was just as turbulent as the rest of the universe.

Not a minute later, her wristcom chimed.

"Bruce," she said, her voice a mix of worry, relief, and annoyance.

"Hey, squeak."

"Seriously?" Frankie had felt her voice dropping back to normal already. Obviously not all the way there yet.

She pushed her comm's volume up, so Spike could listen. "We've been trying to reach you for a day."

"Sorry about that," Bruce's gravel pit of a voice was a warm hug. "Sorry we're still voice only, as well. Still bringing systems online after clearing that bug out.

"At least we're not communicating via hard disk." She heard Bruce snort. "A virus? How?"

"You would not believe." He sounded like he still didn't believe it. "A bug. No, really, a real bug. Specially designed moth, one that likes to chew on input cables. Scamp chewed through a cable and somehow managed to zap itself and its code into our system. It's taken days to get us all straight. And now we have bug zappers in every office."

Frankie tapped the window to see if the little yellow puffy fish would bite. Clever trick. How did Gem put it? Sounds like something Systems Analysis would do. But only for good.

"Well, I'm glad you got it sorted out," she said. The puffy fish did not fall for her feint. "And I've got some news for you, too."

She ran him through the outline of the events at Valdes Underwater Resort. The staged deaths, the witness protection program, and the unlikely alliance between Monica Valdes and the monstrush sharks.

"Incredible," Bruce said. "Impressive. But how long can she keep it up?"

"Could we work with them?" Frankie sat next to Spike. The cyvlossic had walked back and forth across the dome once, and was now splayed on her side on the floor next to Frankie.

"No question we could help them boost the variety of ways for people to fake-die. I'll contact Valdes when the holo is up again and sound her out."

"She was impressed at my cover story. And the video interview. Especially that we have two cyvlossics on the team. Watch out—she thinks it means SystA is loaded!"

Bruce puffed out a breath. Or a snort.

"I can't believe you say it that way."

"Loaded?"

"SystA. It's Sist-Ay."

"Nah, It's sistah. It's your big sister coming in to clean up your mess and stand up to mom and dad for you."

A pause. "You never had a sister did you?" Bruce said.

Frankie set her hand on Spike's shoulder. Well, no. But someday, maybe? Spike couldn't stay cranky forever.

"Anyway," she said. "What are you going to say to the families? The ones that hired you?"

"The ones who did something so bad their own kids wanted to bug out on them?"

"Our clients," Frankie reminded him.

"Nah. We're done with them. If they'll hurt their own children, it's a safe bet they're hurting others. We'll write the report—"

"You mean, lie."

"And they'll pay us the credits. Then they'll be former clients. And we'll use their credits to start looking into them. Valdes might be able to jump start us on that."

Someone spoke off mic.

"Gotta go, Frankie. Good work out there. And Spike too, well done."

"Yeah. First time I feel good about failing."

Despite her wooziness, Spike lifted her head to glare at Frankie. Not a failure, not at all.

"What was that?" Bruce said. "Somebody was talking."

"See you in a week," Frankie said.

She watched life float past, dart past, drift past. The car chimed. Break over.

Frankie bustled back into the limo. Spike did not bustle, but did get in the car. Frankie gave Spike the whole of the forward-facing seat. Frankie stretched her perfectly sized length across the rear-facing one.

With every passing minute, the water pressure eased. She closed her eyes.

Good job, Frankie.

She didn't wake up again until the sunlight streaming through the aircar's windows told her they had emerged from the depths.

Also by Nicky Penttila

Cosmic Weave

Cooperative Realm: Frankie

Cargo Trouble

Frankie Takes a Holiday

Frankie Takes a Dive

Frankie Finds a Dot

Frankie Takes a Bow

Cooperative Realm: Arkhide

Tales of Arkhide

Hidden Planet

The Listeners

The Elders of Arkhide

Historical Fiction

A Note of Scandal

An Untitled Lady

The Spanish Patriot

About the Author

Nicky Penttila wrote her first story, a Mayan murder mystery, in seventh grade. But then came gymnastics, math team, and boyfriends. Later came husband, car payments, and a sleep-depriving work schedule at newspapers across the country. Then came a second career as a science writer. But the fiction kept trickling out, a story here, a novella there, and finally, a real live novel. And she hasn't stopped.

Find more great reads at nickypenttila.com